Pick Your Potion

Witch's Brew Cozy Mystery Book 1

By CC Dragon

The unauthorized reproduction or distribution of this copyrighted work is illegal. Criminal copyright infringement, including infringement without monetary gain, is investigated by the FBI and is punishable by up to 5 years in federal prison and a fine of $250,000.

Please purchase only authorized electronic editions, and do not participate in or encourage the electronic piracy of copyrighted materials. Your support of the author's rights is appreciated.

This book is a work of fiction. Names, characters, places, and incidents either are products of the author's imagination or are used fictitiously. Any resemblance to actual events or locales or persons, living or dead, is entirely coincidental.

Pick Your Potion (Witch's Brew Cozy Mystery 1)
Copyright © February 2017
By CC Dragon
Cover art by Coverkicks.com
Edited by Mary Yakovets
Proofed by: Jessica Bimberg

All rights reserved. Except for use in any review, the reproduction or utilization of this work in whole or in part in any form by any electronic, mechanical or other means, now known or hereafter invented, is forbidden without the written permission of the publisher.

Dedication

For everyone who is hiding their special gifts and talents or just their quirks...Stop it! That's what makes you uniquely you!

Chapter One

I fumbled with the grinder that had, of course, locked up right in the middle of the morning rush. Coffee and tea sounded like such a calming business, but people were serious about their coffee and not patient about waiting for it.

The sighs and mumblings of the backed-up line of customers registered, but I had to focus on the matter at hand or I'd make a mess and it'd only take longer. Magic would help, but there were too many humans watching me far too closely.

"Claudia," my cousin Iris whispered from the back.

I gave her the in-a-minute finger and turned to Brad, one of our new baristas. "Try and get that loose. I'll be right back."

"Right, boss," he said.

Vampires. I liked hiring them, mostly because they took the night shift, lived on expired blood from the blood bank, and their handsome faces brought in the lady customers who ordered the pricier drinks. This one seemed as tame as any of those I employed. But vamps liked structure and following a leader. I was so not that leader. I was a twenty-five-year-old witch with a long line of caffeine deficient customers.

"And make me a green tea with a double shot of calming potion when it gets slow," I said as I wiped my hands on a towel.

Pick Your Potion

Potions were what my aunt cleverly named the shots other places used. Some were just flavor, and others had herbal benefits or vitamin mixes. Our PMS potion might get snickers from men, but the female customers swore by it.

The coffee shop remained a great cover for my coven's deeper purposes. We helped paranormal creatures who didn't want to hurt humans. We could all coexist, or so my hippie aunt believed. She was working the counter in one of her flowing printed dresses, no bra and wicker shoes.

Iris tapped her foot on the floor to get my attention and waved me over faster.

I picked up the pace and joined her. "What's up?"

"Dad has someone in the basement," she said with a twinkle in her eye.

I shrugged and admired the mermaid braid she'd put her honey blonde hair in today. She and her identical twin sister, Violet, were always on trend, even if they were hippies like their mom. Her tank dress flowed in a red paisley today.

"He needs you," she added.

"Why? The cells are free if he needs to lock up anyone," I replied. Hosting any werewolves who needed a secure place during the full moon was also part of the routine.

"I don't think it's that. Please go check. I'll cover for you up here. I don't have a class until ten." She grabbed the towel from my hand.

"Good luck, that grinder likes to spit out grounds." I was sort of happy to be free.

"Every job helps us to help others." Iris smiled.

Her good mood probably had as much to do with cute and eternally youthful Brad as helping people. I wished I could be as cheery and sweet as my cousins about cleaning. I mean, they were like my sisters. My aunt and uncle raised me after my parents died. I was only five when that happened, so I should've taken more of their teaching to heart, but I still had my mom's draw to dark magic and big powers. Strong powers weren't bad, as long as they were used for good. I had to watch the slippery slope.

I didn't have the sweet blonde hair either. I had pure black hair that I jazzed up with a shimmering purple strip to be more like my sisters; they had purplish names, anyway.

I walked down the stairs. The old brick building was full of spirit energy and history. Hartford, Connecticut attracted paranormal creatures because, decades before Salem, it'd had its own witch trials here. That meant witches and paranormal creatures naturally had a right to be here. It also meant we clashed with the local human population, at times.

Owning a coffee shop brought the gossip and the news to me organically. This way, our coven had a finger on the pulse of the human world just in case we needed to push the paranormal further underground for our safety. Witches and wizards were the crossover, after all. Mostly human but with the ability to develop some powers. I had more than my share.

The basement was a maze. Storage was separate. The cages were in the back. There was a small room where vamps or hunters sometimes

Pick Your Potion

crashed when they had nowhere else to go. Uncle Vinny had someone on the cot and was grabbing gauze from the first aid kit.

"What's wrong?" I asked.

"Nothing, he'll be fine. We just need to hide him here for a while," Uncle Vinny replied.

"Sure." I trusted my uncle but still wanted to talk to my guest and feel him out.

My uncle's phone beeped. "I have to take this. Just give him the rundown."

Uncle Vinny took the call and spoke his native language.

I studied the visitor. Mid-twenties, handsome, beat up and scratched but still smug enough to smile and act like he wasn't in pain.

"Ryan Jones," he said.

The Jones was a lie, but most hunters used fake names. "Claudia Crestwood. You're a hunter?" I asked.

He nodded. "What's your uncle speaking? I can't place that language."

"Rom," I said.

"Like Romanian?" Ryan frowned.

"No, like Romani. He's a gypsy. Where are you from?" I asked.

"South Carolina most recently. I was tracking a werewolf that just refused to be contained during the full moon. He kept killing. He killed his family and just didn't care, anymore. He went into a mall just before moonrise. A couple of stores were having midnight sales or staying open around the clock before Christmas for shoppers. I had to take him out. But I was on video. I killed the werewolf, but he turned back into human

4

form once he was dead." He winced and put pressure on his leg.

"I know how werewolves work. So, you got tagged for murder by the local PD?" I tried to assess his wounds. "You need a hospital to check out internal injuries. At the very least you need stitches."

"Nah, just a little rest until things calm down. You're a gypsy witch?" he asked.

"I'm not a gypsy. My aunt is my mother's sister; Vinny married into the family. Sorry, no gypsy blood here. You can stay, but you have to follow the rules." I propped a hand on my hip.

"Sure," he said.

"No meddling in my uncle's cases unless he asks you for backup. No upsetting my coven or my family. Stay out of my coffee shop. Don't upset my customers or the staff."

"No problem. Relax." He grinned.

He was sexy but used to being in control. No doubt I would be a challenge. His broad shoulders and strong arms were tempting, but you had to be tough to be a hunter. Then again, hunters often died young. My uncle had lots of scars, and he was semi-retired. Now, he acted as advisor to the younger hunters in the area.

"That's not all. I have vampires who work here, mostly at night. They have plenty of blood supplied, so they don't kill people. You don't bother them or intimidate them. If you stay for a full moon, I house werewolves. You don't antagonize them." Some hunters liked to keep the fear in the paranormal creatures so they stayed in

Pick Your Potion

line. I've found friendship worked better than threats.

"I only hunt those who've killed humans and refuse to take help in containing themselves." He held up his hands.

The answer was politically correct, but my instinct said he liked the kill. A little more Faith than Buffy.

"I never met a gypsy before. Think he'll take me to stay with them?" Ryan asked.

"Why would he? With that smirk and the flirty attitude you're giving me now… Those guys would beat the crap out of you if you even looked at their daughters. Gypsies are the original hunters. They'd teach you a few lessons." I grabbed the backup first aid kit from the shelf. He'd need it.

"Original hunters?" he asked.

"Think about it. Nomads who traveled light with their families. Men went out and did the work; women stayed home—protecting their kids. It looks old-fashioned, but they all are fighters. The groups were rumored to be associated with poverty, crime, and trouble because they were hunting the creatures that lived in the shadows and hurt humans. That's not an easy life, is it?"

"No, it's not. Makes so much sense. How did I not know that?" He chuckled.

"You do, now. So, respect them and stay away because those guys travel in groups, fight anything bare-handed, and make *The Walking Dead* look like a vacation when they go after someone. From the looks of you, you'd mess with the wrong daughter."

"Then, I'm lucky your dad isn't a gypsy." He grinned.

I shook my head. "You don't know what my dad is. Could be worse than a gypsy. I'll send down some food, coffee, and bottles of water. Don't leave the basement."

Uncle Vinny came back. "Got a plan?"

"He can stay until you patch him up and find another place. I don't want him around the twins too much. You need to make a plan for as soon as he can travel," I said.

"I understand. Think you can heal him?" Uncle Vinny asked.

"Probably, but he needs to be stronger. He's faking strength, right now, but I can feel he's weak. Let Aunt Mandy stitch up the wounds, clean him up, then he can rest. When he's stronger, we'll do a healing session or a few." I texted an order to the sandwich shop next door. Somehow, soup seemed in order, and theirs was the best.

"Okay, I'll tell her. You arrange the food and maybe see if the vamps can spare some clean clothes. He's a mess." Uncle Vinny shook his head.

"It happens. With all the video cameras out there, your job gets harder and harder," I said.

"People see what they want to see on them." Uncle Vinny sighed and headed upstairs.

I shot the young hunter a look. He didn't appear nervous, at all.

"So, what are your powers? Breaking hearts?" he teased.

Pick Your Potion

I shook my head. "Healing, potions, spells, a touch of empathic vibrations—among others."

"Loaded witch. Most of the Wiccans or pagans I meet are all talk," he said.

He wanted a demonstration. "I'm not a magician here to entertain you."

"Impress me. Scare me into obeying all your rules." He winced and grinned too fast to cover his weakness.

The flirtation was a distraction for him. He was trying to forget his pain.

I stared at a dusty bottle of Jack Daniels on the top shelf. There was a ton of coffee and tea stock in the storeroom area, but in here, there were other essentials. I focused and felt the bottle vibrate. I mentally yanked it from the shelf and countered gravity to keep it from freefalling. It floated lower and lower.

Ryan grabbed it and opened it fast. "You're an angel of mercy."

"No, that's my aunt. Be warned, if you make fun of her hippie ways or eccentric style, my uncle will feed you to the werewolves himself. He left the gypsies for her, and they may be different, but they've got the most stable marriage I've ever seen."

"Opposites do attract. Like a hunter and a no-harm doing but powerful witch." He took a slug of whisky.

I tried not to blush. He was hot, even if he was full of himself. "If I have to do harm, I do it. Don't drink too much. Auntie has all natural painkillers that will knock you out and keep you loopy."

"All natural?" he scoffed.

"Cannabis, opium—hell, cocaine is all natural—it's how you distill and use it. She won't get you high, but your pain will be over soon," I said.

"Send her in. But promise you won't take advantage of me while I'm out of it. I want to remember." Ryan blew me a kiss.

I glanced at the bottle in his hand, and it slipped and landed on his very bruised ribs.

"Damn it! Witch!" he shouted.

I walked up as Aunt Mandy was coming down. "He's really in pain, poor dear," she said.

"Don't 'poor dear' him. He's a handful. Thinks he's hotter than hell and twice as tempting."

She shook her head, her blonde hair swinging with her. "I'm sure it's the pain. He's acting tough and covering. The man is being hunted for doing his job and the human world just doesn't understand. I'll take care of him, for now. You get back up there."

"Sure you don't need help? He's strong." I didn't want to help, but seeing Hot Hunter Guy stripped naked wasn't the worst thing in the world. "The twins will fall for his flirting crap."

"They're in college—plenty of normal guys full of crap to flirt with there. If I need someone, Esmerelda can help. You don't need to be around a hunter like him." Aunt Mandy nodded.

"What do mean like him? He's just a human. I lock up werewolves and work with vampires every day," I said.

"This is a stranger. He could take advantage of younger women." She waved at Esme.

9

Pick Your Potion

Esmerelda, in her black cat form, darted down the stairs and sat in the entryway to the concealed rooms. The powerful witch would keep my aunt safe. Esme was deeply connected to the witch world and even taught private lessons to some in the coven. I somehow ended up in between humans and paranormal people.

"You two don't have too much fun." I smiled and let the older ladies get to work with the young fresh meat. My aunt was lying about the stranger, but I didn't push it. We all took turns handling whatever crisis came in the back door.

Esmerelda was the perfect one to keep an eye on him. At one hundred and twenty-five years old, she'd lived most of her life as a cat. In human form, she looked about thirty, but as long as she lived more than half of her life as a cat—she could have all nine lives. She was also a powerful witch—the only one I knew that was stronger than me. I'd wanted to be her since I was a little girl. I loved cats and her power level.

"You okay?" Aunt Mandy asked.

"Yeah, I just don't want him hanging around too long. He likes what he does a little too much. I think." I had no proof, only instinct and years of living with a hunter and meeting tons of them through my uncle.

"Well, if he makes a false move, Esmerelda will turn him into a frog." Aunt Mandy smiled.

"Frog's legs for dinner?" I teased.

"Too far. You so got your mother's sense of humor." Aunt Mandy smacked my shoulder and headed down. "Go upstairs and don't let this hunter play with your mind. Men like this are players, and they look for any opening."

I went up. My aunt often warned me off of bad boy types. My dad probably had that streak, and Aunt Mandy was worried I had my mom's taste in men. The only thing I knew for sure that I got from my father was my hair. My mom had been a dark blonde, but still a blonde. What else did I have from my mysterious dad? It didn't really matter, now. I pushed the tragic history out of my mind, like usual.

Brad handed me my tea.

"Thanks," I said.

The line had gone down with the twins behind the counter. They were experts.

Iris and Violet came over. "Is he cute?"

They were freaky good at being in unison. I envied that they were never alone.

"Cute, full of himself, and dangerous," I said. "Stay away."

"Come on, that's just mean," Violet said.

"It's the truth." I tried to ignore the tingle still running through me. He was a bad boy hunter, and yet, I liked the attention. Thankfully, the twins had too many people looking out for them. "At barely eighteen, you two need to get degrees and careers—not entangled with hunters."

"College boys are no better. They want to screw everything, and then, it's over. At least a hunter risks his life for something that matters. He understands loyalty and dedication," Iris said.

"I'd rather see everyone working to bring the vampires and weres into harmony with humans. We can make it possible for them to be safe and

Pick Your Potion

live with us. I want hunters to have less work." I sipped my tea.

Iris checked her phone. "We better head to class. But you should stay away, Claudia. Really, he's not our type of hunter."

"So?" I asked.

She stared at her phone. "They don't always get gypsy ways or witches. You don't want him to pick up on anything."

Violet bumped her sister. "Pick up on what?"

Iris shook her head. "Nothing. Hunters always want an advantage. This guy doesn't know us or trust us, so keep your guard up, like you told us to do. That's all. Gotta go. Bye."

"Bye," Violet said with a shrug.

"Bye, study!" I called. Iris seemed to know something I didn't. Vi didn't seem to be in on it either. Maybe Iris was being paranoid, but Aunt Mandy had wanted me away from the guy, as well. Why?

"More tea, boss?" Brad asked.

"No, thanks. Do you have any old clothes you'd like to donate? It's for a homeless men's shelter. My aunt said they were low." Lying was part of the game, but Brad might freak and run if he knew a hunter was one floor below him.

"I'll look. I'm on again for the night shift, so I'll bring them by. It's okay if I clock out?" he asked.

"Perfect." I noticed his replacements walking in the door. Lifting my cup in acknowledgement, I took a deep breath. The hunter guy would leave, and a new crisis would pop up. It was all how we handled them.

I noticed my aunt's inspirational quote of the day on the board. *"Cherish now…there won't be another."*

There was no arguing with that. Still, I envied Esmerelda. I'd tried to do the cat thing when I was seven and again at nine. Transfiguring into a cat was just not my area. I left that to Esmerelda and Professor McGonagall. Apparently, you had to start the transfiguring routine before puberty for it to stick and the nine lives to take hold.

Then again, did I want to see this world for the next seven hundred or more years? That seemed daunting. I'd do the best I could and enjoy my time. The crew this shift were all experienced, so I headed up the spiral stairs to our cozy reading nook. Fluffy chairs and sofas flanked shelves of books, much like the first-floor seating area.

We let the regulars go up here when it was crowded on the first floor. There was another room there with all of the coven's needs that was always locked.

I straightened the books and plumped the pillows. A couple of black cats yawned and stretched. They were actual cats; Esmerelda used them as decoys when she turned human. I stroked their fur and found the treat box.

In the midst of my cat time, I heard the raspy voice of Mrs. O'Conner. Petting the cats again, I absorbed their purring vibrations to calm me. Some of our regulars weren't so easy to please—and some, like Mrs. O'Conner, I wished would go to the Starbucks two blocks over.

Pick Your Potion

Chapter Two

Mrs. O'Conner was a regular. A woman in her sixties who wanted things her way. Her bright red wool coat was dusted with snowflakes as she grouched at my barista.

If only my aunt or cousins were working, they knew how to soothe our grumbly customer. She wasn't the only one who was hard to please, but she liked to argue. I sort of admired her; the woman had to be around retirement age, but she was out every day doing something. She came in seven days a week.

"No, not iced!" Mrs. O'Conner snapped.

I reluctantly went down the stairs. The barista was experienced, but the woman never ordered the same drink two days in a row.

"Ma'am, you asked for the spiced cold brew. Did I hear you wrong?" The barista was experienced enough not to take it personally. She was a middle-aged woman who needed to get out of the house once her husband had retired. I hung back to see how they hashed it out.

"Hot. I want the spiced cold brew *hot*." Mrs. O'Conner shrugged.

"Okay. I'm sorry; I didn't hear you say hot." The barista turned back and worked on the odd order.

"I better not be late to work," Mrs. O'Conner said.

Pick Your Potion

"Then, get here earlier." Esmerelda darted up from the basement in human form and grabbed some stuff from behind the counter. She and Mrs. O'Conner snarked at each all the time.

"I'm sorry for the trouble, Mrs. O'Conner. Your drink is on the house," I said.

"What's wrong with it?" Esme rounded the counter and approached as Mrs. O'Conner took the lid off.

"It's iced." Mrs. O'Conner held it out and started to turn.

"I'll take it." Esmeralda got a little too close and bumped our customer's arm. The cold liquid and ice hit Mrs. O'Conner mostly.

"Crap," I whispered to myself.

"You did that on purpose!" Mrs. O'Conner snapped.

"No, I was trying not to waste a perfectly good drink. I'm sorry." Esme grabbed a towel from a barista and handed it to Mrs. O'Conner.

"Can everyone calm down, please?" I nudged Esmerelda. "You have work to do."

"Fine. Send down coffee when you can." Esme stalked off.

I took the iced coffee and threw it away. "We'll pay for the dry cleaning."

"I hope I don't catch a cold from this chill. I should get my nephew to sue you." She took the hot cup of coffee.

"For a chill?" I asked. "Would free coffee for a month make this up to you?"

"It's a start. I should find a real coffee shop, not some little witchy joke. Potions," she scoffed.

"If you get the Starbucks app, you can order ahead, and they have it in writing," I suggested.

She glared at me. "You want me to go elsewhere?"

"I want my customers to be happy. This shop is an alternative to the chains. There's a Dunkin Donuts in the other direction. They have an app, too. We have potions and customize drinks. More flavors. More blends. You might need some calming tea instead of coffee, but that's your choice." I had a wide variety of customers. College kids who wanted to be counter culture. Hipsters who rejected the prestige of the brands...at times. People with illnesses came in for customer brewed healing teas from my aunt.

As long as we covered our bills, I was happy. I wasn't about competition with the big chains. Losing one customer who made others uneasy wasn't going to upset me that much.

She shook a crooked finger at me. "You'll never see me here, again."

When the door closed, some of the customers clapped. I sighed and saw the relief in the smiles of my baristas. There were plenty of places to grab coffee.

"Everyone in line gets a free biscotti or muffin for the wait. I'm running next door to get some soup and stuff. There's a friend staying the basement spare room," I said.

The baristas would find out eventually when they needed supplies.

I swung into the soup and sandwich place that opened early for breakfast sandwiches.

Pick Your Potion

"Hi, Claudia, your order is ready." Fred was a sweet guy pushing thirty. His shop had homemade bread and soups. The smell alone made me give up the idea of ever going no carb.

"Thanks. Can you add a couple of grilled cheeses and a turkey, ham and Swiss to those? Plus a couple pints of the potato soup?" I might as well get lunch for me, Aunt Mandy, and Esme since they'd be tired from working on the hunter.

"Anything for you." He went to work. "They say there's a snowstorm coming. You ready?"

"Always ready. It's New England." I shrugged. "Soup weather. Business good?"

I had vamps to shovel the sidewalk, and they didn't mind the cold. I had an awesome collection of knee high and thigh high boots with soles that gripped well. I was tall enough; heels weren't necessary. I liked heels, but in winter, I could leave them.

"Business is good. I wish I had some ancestral witch connection to market like you do. It's genius. The witch's brew." He complimented me on the name of my shop all the time. But about business. He had the oddest ways of flirting I'd even seen. The guy was nice, good-looking, hardworking, but human. No wizard potential. No power.

Probably what I should be looking for, only it did nothing for me.

He hit buttons on the cash register display. "And the friends and family discount," he said so I could hear.

"You don't have to do that," I said, just like every other time.

18

"We small businesses have to stick together. You've got coffee chains surrounding you. I've got all sorts of sandwich shop chains. Subway has soups, now. We will survive. My grandparents opened this shop." He looked around fondly.

"I know we'll survive. Come by for some coffee later, on the house. You can't live on soup," I teased him.

"Thanks. I just give you a discount; you give it away." He took my credit card and ran it through.

I signed the slip, put my card away, grabbed my big order and headed for the door. I could've gotten it myself, but there was Fred opening the door for me.

"Thanks." I left and really wished I could tell Fred that I was a serious witch. Humans just weren't my thing. I wanted to be a powerful witch, and a guy without powers seemed dull. Of course, the flip side was that power sometimes tempted people to the dark magics.

A powerful wizard with a sense of right and wrong; was that so hard to find? Maybe it was.

I surrounded myself with ethical checks and touchstones to keep me from enjoying my powers too much that I crossed that imaginary line to the dark.

A customer held the door for me, and I slipped inside. "Thanks."

Aunt Mandy was taking a tea break and grabbed some of the bags. We headed in the back behind the counter through the door to the kitchen. There was a break room there, as well as the usual dishwashers and sinks.

"How's he doing?" I asked.

Pick Your Potion

"More hurt than he'll admit. I think he needs more than one healing session. There must be internal injuries." She collected some food and other essentials. She took Esme's food, as well.

"Esme can come up and eat," I said.

"She wants to keep an eye on him. He's tried to break free twice. She had to put a spell on him twice. He wants to leave," she said.

"Let him," I replied.

"He's hurt. I think he's afraid of witches, quite honestly. Most hunters have had a bad para experience that drives them to keep the peace and seek justice," she said.

"And some just like an excuse to kill," I added.

"He says you treated him like a prisoner," she said.

"He's full of crap. Scared and lashing out. Get going or your grilled cheese will be cold." I unwrapped my meat heavy sandwich.

Another thing my hippie aunt couldn't convert me to: vegetarianism. I found paper bowls for the soup and poured myself some. I grabbed a fruity mixer drink from the fridge that turned out to be a sample of a new flavor. Strawberry Kiwi Grape with some green tea extract.

Aunt Mandy returned with a stern look.

"What did I do, now? I'm just sitting here." She might as well be my mom. Part of me still felt bad for my teenage years when that was my go to excuse for being a bit wild and rebellious.

"Esme says Mrs. O'Conner wasn't happy today."

"She only likes you or the twins. The woman is hard to please. Normally, they get it right, but Esme is the one who splashed the coffee on her. Iced coffee, thankfully." I didn't want to think about the hot coffee lawsuit threats.

"She needs to rest. She needs some cat time. I've worked her too hard this morning." Aunt Mandy grabbed a juice and sat down.

"She's a really strong witch." I rolled my eyes.

"And that hunter was in really bad shape. Still is. He could've bled out. Vin should've taken him to the hospital." She took a bite of her grilled cheese, and it helped her relax.

"I told him that. I didn't examine the guy too closely—he was all flirty and weird. But those leg wounds..." I shrugged.

"Herbs and magic can't solve everything. Maybe he tangled with more than one werewolf. Is that why you think he's not being totally truthful?" my aunt asked.

I added crackers to my soup. "I don't know. He's not local. He needs to go back where his people are," I said.

"He tracked the werewolf through the Carolinas, but if he goes back, they'll arrest him. Let Vin manage him." Aunt Mandy finished off her sandwich and started on some soup.

"He tends to take on more than he should and help other hunters. He needs to find some home for wayward hunters and park this guy there." I took a big bite of my sandwich.

My aunt eyed the sandwich. "You don't mind helping werewolves. Why resist helping hunters?"

Pick Your Potion

"They're human. They have everyone out there to help them. I get he's running from a charge that isn't fair, but he can go to the hospital here. Where he can be treated in the best way. Then, he could move on. He's far enough away from the scene of the crime. He's a drain on us and trouble," I said.

"Your uncle was trouble back in the day." She smiled like a schoolgirl in love.

"What made you and Mom want to marry hunters?" I asked.

She went a bit pale and took a drink of her juice. "I was intrigued by the gypsy culture. I thought it was just expanding my horizons with friends, but it turned into more. Vin has a good code of ethics. Not all hunters do, I admit it."

"And my dad?" I asked.

"Well, he wasn't a gypsy. Your mom met him through Vin. Hunters are always running into each other on a case. Your dad handled some very dangerous vampire nests. He always tried to get the lone ones to accept help. Your mom was trying to find a way to give that help. I mean, she had the potion for werewolves not to turn. But vampires needed to feed. It took time. You've advanced their goals. But we all take a risk," she said.

It was nothing I hadn't heard before. She never gave too many details. I'd asked many times over the years for more info, but it upset her. She lost her sister; I lost my parents. For me, it was a blurry memory of a big black werewolf. She'd lost her friend since childhood. I hated to push and upset her.

22

"Risk like that hunter. Next time Mrs. O'Conner comes in, I'll make sure you serve her. It's the only way to keep her happy," I said.

"Esme said she won't be back," Aunt Mandy replied.

"She always comes back. I offered her free coffee for a month. She'll be back in a day or two, complaining about the other places." I laughed.

"Normally, I'd agree with you, but Esme seemed very pleased and sure of her prediction. I should go relieve her. Let her get a real nap without keeping one eye on that kid," she said.

"I'll clean up, check on things out front, and then start the healing potion." I took a drink of my fruit mixer.

"Good. But I agree with what you said earlier today. Keep the twins away from him. You should avoid him, too," Aunt Mandy said.

"Why me?" I asked. "Iris acted the same way. Like I should avoid him. What's the problem? What don't I know?"

My aunt swallowed hard. "I don't know what she meant. You tend to take on the toughest jobs, and perhaps, she thinks you need a break. Have some fun. Esme can babysit him. She's seen men flirt for over a century. Nothing will get by her."

"I thought Esme took on some more witches for her private magic tutoring. She's got to be busy with them. Plus, he's in my shop. I have to be able to handle him if he acts up in the night." I shrugged.

"I know, and of course you can in a pinch. He's just the type who wants all the attention he can get, and he'll play games. Don't feed that. The

Pick Your Potion

vampires can overpower him if he acts up. Just lock him up. Esme may have more clients, but she'll always make time for you." Aunt Mandy patted my arm.

"Lock him up? What have you done with my hippie, always kind aunt who thought locking the cats out of the café level was cruel?" Something wasn't adding up.

She smiled weakly. "I want to trust everyone, but your instincts said you didn't trust him. I believe in your instincts. We need to help him but not let him cause trouble in our lives. Everything is connected, and he could cause waves of good or storms of bad. As soon as he shows signs of the bad, he must be contained. The cages are safe for werewolves—there's nothing dangerous about locking the cage to be sure he does what Vin thinks is best. Young hunters are impulsive and rash. He could run off too soon and get hurt again or an infection take over because he's weak. It's for his own good. Sometimes, we have to do bad things for the greater good."

I knew when to stop arguing. "That's quite a speech. Fine, if he acts up, the cage. The vamps will put him there. Just the odd well check and food delivery."

"Vamps can do that, too. I don't think we need to get too close to this hunter," she said.

"You don't want any of your girls marrying hunters?" I teased.

She waved me off with a chuckle and grabbed another juice before she left.

I left a note for our overnight baristas, who had the most free time to mix up a new blend of fruit mixer. The strawberry kiwi was too sweet. It needed more of a blackberry undertone, even with the grape in the mix.

For now, I had to mix a powerful potion. They weren't the most glamorous part of the witch world, but they packed a punch. I debated adding a backup potion of *cat got your tongue* to the main one. Shutting up that hunter would help calm things down tremendously.

Pick Your Potion

Chapter Three

Walking into the coven room on the second floor, I locked the door behind me. The smell of sage and other herbs ignited the witch in me. Soothing customers and keeping my aunt happy were part of my life, but magic was my purpose.

The paranormal world felt more natural to me. Part of me would love to ignore reality and the humans, but that's how problems start. Too often, paranormal creatures would avoid humans and eventually let their guard down.

Grabbing a small cauldron, I assessed what ingredients I'd need. I gathered everything for a healing potion and began to mix it. The sooner he was healed, the sooner he could get on with his life. But my aunt said he was really injured. Should I make this potion extra strong? Then, he might push himself, and he'd relapse.

He needed to sleep more than anything. I added herbs to encourage sleeping. Once everything was in, I cleaned up. Taking the cauldron with me, I locked the room and headed down the stairs.

Sure, I got a few odd looks, carrying a straight up cauldron, but the café was called Witch's Brew. Some thought it was a joke or a nod to the old witch trials. Others knew that my aunt was part of the Wiccan religion. As long as she didn't recruit, no one seemed to care.

Pick Your Potion

I headed straight downstairs and found Aunt Mandy forcing tea on the hunter. Esme sat in the corner in cat form, swishing her tail back and forth.

"Is he cooperating?" I asked.

"I'll do anything you say," he teased.

"How much have you had to drink?" I asked.

"Not much. But your aunt's pain medication is wonderful." He smiled.

"That's so you can rest. The healing will take days," my aunt replied.

Esme darted under his cot and batted out a phone. One of those pay-as-you-go burner phones a lot of hunters used to make themselves harder to trace.

"Look at this. Who did you need to call?" I asked Ryan.

"I have friends. I needed to touch base. The cops are still looking for me. Can't go back. Sorry," he said with a smirk.

"This will help." I set the cauldron down.

Esme dashed off into another area and returned in human form wearing a long dress but no shoes.

"I heard you had a problematic customer. I could take care of that for you. Ladies love me." He laughed.

"How much did you give him?" I asked my aunt.

"He was in a lot of pain when we cleaned the wounds." She shrugged.

Esme cleared her throat. "The customer won't return. I've seen it."

"I think she might with that free coffee offer," I said.

"I can't explain it, but my visions are rarely wrong," Esme said.

I knew she was right.

"Who is dumb enough to mess with witches? You could turn her into a frog," he said.

"I could turn you into a frog. Keep you in a cage—it'd be less trouble." I grinned.

"And miss all this?" He gestured to his body.

He was hot. They'd left him shirtless and in nothing but boxers. The wounds were extensive and all over. Deep gashes. The werewolf or wolves had gotten a hold of him for some time.

"You're lucky to be alive. You need to sleep, eat, get your bandages changed, and go back to sleep." I held up the cauldron.

"That sounds boring," he said.

Esmerelda mixed the potion and nodded. We whispered the spell over it then poured it into his glass. My aunt helped him get the glass to his lips.

He got half of the potion down. "That tingles. You ladies are too strong to let some human complain and ruin your business."

"She didn't ruin our business. And you're a human, so should we not help you?" I asked.

"I'm a hunter. I know all about you. I help keep the humans from going crazy and attacking the paranormal world by weeding out the evil ones like rabid dogs."

My aunt pushed the second half of the potion on him.

"We'd rather everyone get along, but you are a necessary evil, for now," I said.

Pick Your Potion

"You don't like me because I know too much about you witches. But you shouldn't let regular clueless humans push you around. You're strong." He gulped down the rest of it.

"I'm strong enough to put you in your place if you need it. Esmerelda could smoke you into nothing with no effort." I smiled at her.

"Don't forget it." She pointed at him.

"You're very strong. I want to help you if I can. I like you ladies." He snuggled up with the pillow and reached out.

He grabbed my hand.

"No, grabby," I said.

"I expected more of a hands-on healing." He pouted.

Esme slapped him across the face. "You're doped up enough now that we can sew up the cuts, and that potion will help you."

"Yeah, if you grab or touch anyone, I'll have the vampires toss you out in the snow and drain you if you try to get back in. I don't like gropey guys," I warned him.

"You gave me all this. I'm used to pain, not drugs," he admitted.

"Maybe I did overdo it," Aunt Mandy admitted.

"No, don't blame yourself. He should be at a hospital, not here. We can put him in a cage or tie his hands to the cot," I suggested.

Esme nodded and waved her hand. Rope appeared and tightly knotted his wrists to the metal sides of the cot.

"You think this will hold me?" He smirked.

30

"It'll slow you down if you want to grab someone. If you want to leave, we'll let you go," I offered.

"I'm not a good guest. I'm a lone wolf." He laughed and howled.

I looked up. We didn't need him freaking out the customers. "You're tripping. No more pain meds. Maybe I should take your phone while you're out of it."

"No! I'm not a prisoner. I appreciate you letting me stay here, but I need to stay in touch with my friends and other hunters. I have to know what's going on with my case." He clutched the phone.

"He'll be less happy soon." My aunt got out a suture kit.

"You know what you're doing?" he asked.

"I've sewn up my husband plenty." My aunt pulled a chair up. "It's really just his leg that needs it. I can tape the others together."

"Fine." I glared at the hunter. "Don't give up your location. I'm not an accessory to anything."

"I'd never endanger my helpers." He hissed when my aunt stuck a needle in his skin.

"Just a little local numbing," she said.

I turned to Esme. "You can go. I'll watch him." Esme nodded and headed upstairs.

"Don't worry. I won't lay a hand on your aunt. Her husband would kill me," he said.

"Not if I get you first. And I hide bodies better than hunters do." I tossed the cup he'd been drinking from in the air. With a flick of my fingers, it was gone in a puff of smoke.

"Hot," he said.

Pick Your Potion

"Men." I shook my head. All the good-looking ones were evil, human, or stupid. This guy was two out of three. I wasn't convinced which two yet, but time would reveal all.

Chapter Four

Running into the darkness, I dared to glance back. I couldn't see the werewolf, but I heard the snarls and howls. I ran faster until my heart felt like it would explode in my chest. Finally, I found a tree and transfigured into a cat. I climbed the tree and went as high as I could without breaking a branch.

The sounds seemed to be coming closer. That only made the terror worse. It sounded like a pack was surrounding me.

"No!" I shouted as I sat up in bed. Even knowing it was a dream didn't stop the fear.

I hadn't had those dreams in a while. The cold sweat made me shiver, but I threw off the covers, anyway. It had to be the presence of the hunter.

The dreams had plagued me when I was young. As the memory of my mother's death faded, I just had nightmares about being chased by a werewolf myself. It didn't matter that my uncle had killed the werewolf that murdered my parents.

In this dream, I felt like I was chasing a secret. Maybe it was whatever my aunt and Iris were talking around. Hunters had never been a sore point, before but we'd never known any but gypsy hunters as far back as I could remember. I didn't really remember my dad... He was the only non-gypsy hunter I knew of. They were rare and not

Pick Your Potion

trusted in gypsy circles. Nothing clicked. The puzzle was giving me a headache.

I trudged to the bathroom and washed my face. My little loft apartment on the top floor was perfect for me. Open space done in dark greens and dark purples. I could be myself here. But the idea that there was a hunter in the basement of the building made me anxious.

Hunters were a necessary evil. Some vampires and werewolves always refused to coexist peacefully. The vamps wanted real hot blood from a human. The werewolves needed to hunt and experience their wolfie side. Or so they claimed.

Killing humans or other vampires or werewolves, that was murder. They had to be held accountable, and there was no prison to hold them. Human justice wasn't aware enough or evolved enough to understand the needs. No vampire or werewolf council existed to judge them or set down laws. The witch's council was a reassuring international body that brought order for us. The hunter problems were relatively few when they were gypsy hunters. They had their own way of keeping order. But the rogue non-gypsy hunters were more dangerous.

On the flip side, some hunters were too into their work and judged unsafe. What was to stop them from someday rising up against witches? If Ryan decided I was too powerful, would he kill me?

What had kept them in check was their loner lifestyle. They had a loose network, but they called on each other only in emergencies. At least, those were the non-Romani hunters. The gypsy hunters had a network and could easily wage a war, but they respected the right of the paranormal to live. The Nazis had tried to exterminate the gypsies, so the gypsies were not about to treat others that way.

No, the loner hunters worried me more.

I checked my phone to see if there were any issues or problems. It sucked that I slept so hard I'd never hear my text notification. Luckily, my family and staff knew to call me, not just text, if they really needed me.

Brad had texted that he'd brought the clothes for donation.

Damn!

I ran my fingers through my hair and checked in a mirror that the bedhead wasn't too awful. Finding the jeans I'd worn today on the floor, I slid them back on. I'd fallen asleep in my pink T-shirt that had the café's name on it, so I stepped into my fuzzy black cat slippers and headed downstairs.

Brad and the other baristas all wore shirts in various colors with the same logo. I liked my little coffee shop, especially now when it was quiet. Some college kids and night owls occupied tables, but there was no rush or unhappy customers.

I slid behind the counter, and Brad handed me a bag.

"Thanks," I said.

"No problem. It's quiet tonight. But rumor is you've got a guest," Brad said.

Pick Your Potion

He leaned on the counter and then shifted his posture and wiped a towel across the prep area. The fidgeting told me he was uneasy.

"Have you heard anything from downstairs? He's supposed to stay down there," I said.

Brad shook his head. "Nothing. I just don't like the feel of him. The smell," he said.

Vampires' heightened senses were annoying, but it meant I never smelled burnt coffee. They always caught it first. But it made them jumpy if there was someone they didn't like the sense of.

"I'll check on him. He's injured so you could take him out easily. You're faster than humans, anyway," I said.

He nodded.

The blood. No wonder Brad was jumpy. He could smell the dried blood on Ryan's clothing. Even though they'd cleaned up and bandaged his wounds, his clothes were still there.

"Are you eating enough? I know the blood bank stuff isn't as good as fresh stuff, but with my aunt's supplements and some extra blood, you'll be fine." I patted his arm.

He nodded. "It's just tempting. Some hunters aren't so nice, and if I were to feed from a human again…"

"I hear ya, but don't." I wagged a finger at him. "I could eat nothing but candy or try meth. But that's not good for me. Killing humans hurts you."

"There are parties where humans let you drink. You don't kill them, just feed," he said.

"Creepy. And how long do you think you could just feed without going out for a kill the next day?" I asked.

"I understand what you're saying. But you eat meat," he said.

"I do. And if you want to stop the blood bank and go for pig's blood, there's a butcher up the street. Some vampires prefer that. It's fresher and not processed. Heat it up and go for it. You've got options, but if you kill a human or a cat, I'll stake you myself."

He grinned sheepishly. "I won't. But the blood smell—"

"I'll handle it." I took the bag with me downstairs.

"I thought I heard your voice." Ryan was up and waiting for me.

"Feeling better?" I asked as I pulled a worn pair of jeans and a pair of sweatpants from the bag. Digging for more, I retrieved a few T-shirts and set it all on his cot.

"Good enough. I'll need some of your aunt's magic in the morning." He sat up slowly.

"Change into these. I'll wash your clothes." I grabbed his jacket from the corner. His shirt was on the other side of the room. I found his pants under the bed.

"I'm not wearing another guy's underwear." He tossed the new clothes aside.

"I don't care if you go commando or stay down here naked. Those are your clothing options. These blood-encrusted rags need to be washed or the vamps will down here for a snack." I smiled.

Pick Your Potion

He slid off the boxers, and I tried not to look. He was well-defined and muscled. I grabbed his boxers and turned for the stairs.

"Running away so soon?" he teased.

"I'm not running. I want the vamps to calm down, though. The sooner these are in the washer with a lot of soap, the better for you." I shot him a look.

He grunted and winced as he tugged on the sweatpants. "I'm decent."

"That's debatable," I mumbled.

"What?" he asked.

"Nothing. Did you pull that bandage off your leg?" I asked.

"No. It's tender but not bleeding through or anything. Wouldn't want to tempt your friends," he said.

"You don't want fight them off. Not in your condition. My aunt probably needs to get you on some natural antibiotic herbs to avoid infection." I moved closer and put my hand to his forehead. "Yeah, feels like you've got a fever."

"I'm fine. Just having hot dreams about you." He grabbed my wrist.

"That's cute. You're not that hot or charming. You're sick, and we're trying to help you."

He sighed. "You said you didn't care if I left. Now, you care?"

"No, but my uncle does. If you cooperate and appreciate the help, fine. I'm not going to turn you out to die or land in jail for doing your job. But don't test me."

"You've sent people to their death? I've killed. I've looked vamps in the eye and staked them," he said.

"And I haven't? I hire vamps. Not every one of them can handle being tame. If my employee slips, I stake them. Or however I see fit. That's my responsibility."

"Tough girl. I thought you'd make your uncle handle it," he said.

"My uncle saved my life when I was kid. I trust him, and I'll help. But I take care of my own messes. You don't want to be one of them." I poked him in the chest with my shimmering purple nail.

"No, I don't. But I can enjoy the cat-and-mouse game. Do you turn feline like Esmerelda?" he asked.

"Not as a rule. I can transfigure, at times, but I didn't achieve that young enough to get the nine lives ticket." I wasn't proud of that.

"Maybe you're more of a dog person. Ever tried being a cute little poodle?" he teased.

"Please," I scoffed. "I'm going. Aunt Mandy will check on you in the morning with breakfast."

"Night," he said.

I trudged up the stairs with the bloody clothes and went right for the washer off the kitchen area in the back. Lots of scented detergent, long presoak, heavy wash, and a note on the washer that said *Private load—see Claudia before opening*.

They could think it was my sexy lingerie or witch's robes. I just didn't want the vamps to open

Pick Your Potion

it up if all the blood didn't come out in the first wash.

Brad was waiting for me when I stepped back into the café area.

"The clothes are in the wash. Spray some air freshener and brew some of the gingerbread blend. That has a strong scent," I suggested.

He nodded. "You're sure he's a good hunter?"

"My uncle brought him here. He's injured enough to not be a threat, now. But I'll try to check into the case he's running from to be sure. But it was a werewolf case, and with all the video surveillance, you know hunters are getting hunted by the human police, now," I said.

"Okay. I can defend myself, but I don't like the idea of you alone here with him." He folded his arms.

"Aww, that's sweet. But I'm not. The shop is always open with staff. Plus..." I held out my hand. The huge knife they used to cut up fruit for our mixers flew from the counter to my hand. "I think I'm good."

He nodded and took the knife.

"Good work, everyone. I'm heading back to bed," I said.

The baristas on night shift did the more intense cleaning and restocking. One stayed on the register, just in case. They murmured some sort of response but were all engrossed in their tasks.

As I climbed the stairs, I could smell the blood and sweat from Ryan's clothes clinging to my shirt. *Yuck*. As soon as I closed and locked the door to my apartment behind me, I stripped naked and headed for the shower.

Pick Your Potion

Chapter Five

Two days later, I didn't really want to face the morning. The day before, the hunter was shivering with infection. My offers to take him to urgent care or the ER were met with glares. My aunt's antibiotic potions always worked on me, but if we'd missed some sort of internal injury or deeper infection...

I'm a witch, not a doctor!

I came down to supervise the morning rush and make myself a morning jolt with a double calming potion.

"Mrs. O'Conner still hasn't been back," said the head barista for the shift.

"She wasn't in yesterday either," Esmerelda said.

"Don't worry about her. It might take a week or two, but she gets sick of the chain stores." I straightened up a bit behind the counter then took my coffee to a quiet corner.

Esmerelda followed me. "You doubt my vision? We won't see her again."

"Okay. She'll find another café she likes better. Do you think our business is in trouble?" I asked.

She shook her head. "I think we just need a couple of signs. *If we get your drink wrong, the right one is free.* Another that says *Hot drinks are scalding, cold drinks are frigid...sip at your own risk.* Funny but cover our butts."

Pick Your Potion

"All the cups are stamped with the warning that contents are served very hot." I did see the humor in her approach. "But those are funny. Why not?"

"I'll paint some up." Esme nodded.

"Maybe one that says *Our baristas are only human. If you wish to curse and yell, the owner is a real witch! Please see her.*" I laughed.

"Love it." Esme smiled.

"How is the guest today?" I asked.

Esme's smile faded fast. "He's a pain. Apparently, there was a cut in a private area. We let him have some privacy. Well, he didn't have it cleaned and treated properly, so that's the infection. Not your aunt's fault, though she's blaming herself. Like she was going to judge his thing."

"Are we sure this werewolf he took out wasn't his ex-girlfriend?" I joked.

"It is an odd place for a fight injury. Your aunt is on the case now and smearing him head to toe with her enhanced witch hazel. That should help."

"I just can't believe he's worse. I was hoping to be rid of him soon." I sipped my coffee.

The bell over the door rang, and I glanced over. A man and a woman dressed in suits walked in and surveyed the place. Esmerelda stared at them. If she were in cat form, her back would be arched and she'd be hissing.

"What?" I asked.

"I'm going down to help your aunt." She left calmly but quickly.

I looked back at the couple. They cut the line and flashed a badge at my head barista, who

44

pointed me out. I took a long drink of my coffee. Was it Ryan? I had been visited once before by the police when a new hire had a sketchy past.

The duo approached me.

"Ms. Crestwood? I'm Detective Keller; this is Detective Shelley. We need to speak to you in private," said the male cop.

"Sure. Let's go into my office. Would you like something to drink?" I offered as I refilled my cup with black coffee from the refill station.

"No, thank you," he replied.

I added some cream and a packet of raw sugar. As we walked to the door marked *Private,* I stirred my coffee. I didn't want to alarm any of the staff so I didn't ask all the questions in my head until I closed the door behind them.

They took the two guest chairs as I settled behind the desk. Normally our accountant was the only whom ever used this office. I wasn't a desk type but there were times when privacy and professionalism were needed.

"How can I help you?" I asked.

"We were made aware of an incident that occurred here a couple of days ago. A customer of yours had coffee spilled on her?" Detective Shelley asked.

I hid my relief that it wasn't about Ryan. "Iced coffee, yes. The customer was offered towels. It's not like hot coffee. And she removed the lid; someone bumped into her. We offered to pay for her dry cleaning, her order was free, and she has free coffee for a month. I don't think I could've done more for a relatively minor incident."

Pick Your Potion

"You know this customer?" Detective Keller asked.

"She's a regular. Sometimes, she gets annoyed and goes elsewhere for a week or two. But we're the best."

"She's a regular, but your barista got her order wrong?" Detective Shelley asked.

"She changed her order every day to suit her mood. She'd cycle between five different coffee drinks. Cold or hot, depending on the season. The barista misheard that she wanted the drink iced. She really went to the police over a little spilled coffee and a wrong order?" I leaned back in my chair.

"Was she a problem customer?" Detective Keller asked.

"She was particular. Not always pleasant, but some people are bears before they've had their caffeine. Nothing we're not used to. We always made it right if something was wrong. She'd threaten to never come back before. I'd give her a week or a month of free coffee, and she'd come back. I fully expected to see her next week." I couldn't believe she'd file a complaint. "What sort of complaint did Mrs. O'Conner file?"

"She didn't. Mrs. O'Conner was found dead at her home yesterday morning. Her husband was unable to wake her." Detective Keller sounded as if he was reading the news of the day.

"Dead?" A chill ran down my spine. "I'm sorry. I didn't think she was that old."

"She wasn't. Late sixties. However, she was a brittle Type 1 diabetic. She had some health issues as a result, as well as being insulin dependent."

"Well, as long as it was natural causes. I'm sorry to hear about it. I'm not sure what I can do other than extend the free coffee to her family." I felt awful for Mrs. O'Conner, but why were the police bothering with a coffee shop?

"Her husband is not convinced it was natural causes. She had spoken to him during the day about how upset she was by your shop. He's convinced someone did something to harm her or that the extreme stress hastened her death. We're visiting all the places she was the day before she passed, to be sure. You didn't notice anything odd? Did she look ill?" Detective Shelley asked.

"No, not at all. She was feisty as ever. On her way to her job at the library, I believe. She was very active and came in nearly every day. Only brought her husband in a few times." I shrugged.

"Did he like your shop?" Detective Keller asked.

"You'd have to ask him. He said he liked his coffee black and cheap from the pot at home. Mrs. O'Conner said he was military so he'd gotten used to black coffee that was bitter swill. He had no use for tea or fancy coffee drinks. She liked the variety," I replied.

"Did she make any other threats besides not returning?" asked Detective Kelly.

"Not that I remember. People say things when they're upset. We try hard to be a good part of everyone's morning. We know they're going off to work or school, and even stay-at-home moms need fuel to handle little ones. They want to be on time and have their coffee right. It might seem like nothing compared to solving crime, but a bad

Pick Your Potion

experience here can ripple through their day. I'm sorry if we gave Mrs. O'Conner a bad last day." I still couldn't fully process that she was gone.

"Did she frequently make comments about you being a witch or Wiccan? About the name of the shop?" Detective Keller asked.

"Oh, that. No, she didn't mention it much. She'd been a customer for a couple years, now. She complained more when we got a new barista, because she expected them to get everything wrong or they were slower. We tried never to let her have a trainee. This time, I think she was just looking for things to complain about, because we'd done everything to fix the wrong order and spilled coffee. People lash out at the Witch's Brew name, but there were witch trials in Hartford before Salem. It's part of the history and a good hook." I smiled.

Detective Shelley smiled back. "It is. Most people speak highly of your place. Better pricing and service. Welcoming feel."

"That's nice to hear," I said.

"What are these potions on your menu?" Detective Keller asked.

"Those are just a cute themed name for shots like a shot of hazelnut flavor. We have some vitamin, herbs, antioxidants, fruits, and unique flavor mixes. To keep with the theme, my aunt thought calling them potions was a fun way to stand out. Everything is perfectly safe. We have ingredient pamphlets, and it's on our website." I opened a drawer and handed them a pamphlet. They weren't the first to wonder what was in a potion. Like we were secretly selling drugs or

48

something... I wasn't sure what they doubted, but there was nothing that'd get me in trouble.

"Thank you," Detective Shelley said as she took the paper.

"So, nothing happened here that could've caused her health issues?" Detective Keller asked.

"I'm not a doctor. I'm sure her blood pressure was up from being upset. If she was in any distress, we would've called an ambulance. She walked out of here like she owned the place," I said.

"Did she have words here with anyone specific? You? The barista who served her? Others?" Detective Shelley asked.

"A friend, Esmerelda. She went to get the wrong beverage and bumped into Mrs. O'Conner. No one here was out to get her or hurt her. I'm sorry she's gone, but I don't know what we can do for you." I felt like they were circling something but not getting to the point.

"We need to speak to the baristas on duty that morning. As well as this Esmerelda. Just like we're speaking to you. Mr. O'Conner is convinced that someone hurt his wife, and that it was not natural causes." Detective Keller frowned.

"If he didn't insist, is that what you'd assume it was?" I asked.

"A woman of her age and with those health issues, our ME feels the odds are it was natural. Now, he will be performing an autopsy, and there will be a tox screen. They're a little backed up from the holidays, but they'll get to it," replied Detective Shelley.

Pick Your Potion

"I'm sorry. I understand Mr. O'Conner is upset. She was very active, but we never know when our time is up." I wrote down the staff working that morning.

"So, you didn't take her threats about Wiccans or witches seriously?" Detective Keller asked.

"We've had the odd protester over the years. People don't mind witch talk at Halloween, but around Easter, we get a few people who need to make a statement. Generally, we talk to them and show we're not Satan worshippers or anything like that. We have an old belief system, and the point of reminding people that witch trials happened here is so we never have that sort of thing happen, again. We tolerate all religions and races and types of people here. We're more like nature-loving hippies in a way. We just want to be tolerated. That and some free coffee usually gets them to go home." I smiled.

"Is there any one of your coven or staff that might take that threat personally? Someone new, maybe?" asked Detective Shelley.

I rolled over the question in my mind. Esme would be the only one to take it personally, but she wasn't new. She'd never take anything Mrs. O'Conner said to heart, anyway. "No. She was an older woman who was having a bad morning. I train my staff to ignore the moods and the attitudes and focus on the coffee order. Get it right, and the rude customers go away; the happy customers are happier. Get the orders right, and they are rewarded by us. Tipping for coffee is still very hit or miss."

50

The detectives shared a look.

"What?" I asked.

"In these circumstances, we would do a courtesy death investigation. Mr. O'Conner is adamant someone did something. His wife was active, taking care of her health, and her doctor confirmed she was doing reasonably well. Of course, her body was worn harder by the diabetes. She'd had some issues already." Detective Keller consulted his notes.

"I understand. I wrote down the names of the baristas working. Esmerelda is here, now. She's a regular and a member of my coven. She helps when we need it. Beyond that, I'm not sure how to help you. I certainly hope it all proves to be natural causes, and the family can grieve in peace." There was more. They weren't telling me something. They didn't want to tell me something critical.

"Wonderful." Detective Shelley took the list.

"We'll be back to talk, again, I'm sure. You can keep going business as usual but understand that we might have more questions or want to inspect your equipment," he said.

"If the equipment had been tampered with, more people would've been made ill. No one has complained, and I drink something made by our baristas every day to be sure they are doing things right. If everything hasn't been cleaned, I can tell. Quality control." I tapped my coffee cup.

"Still, if we find more reasons to suspect murder over natural causes—we can get a warrant, and we can take anything we need. Let's hope the ME gets caught up on things sooner so

Pick Your Potion

we can put this to bed. Until then, don't leave the state," Detective Keller said.

"What? Wait. I'm a suspect?" That's crazy!

"It's just a precaution," Detective Shelley said.

"No, why am I a suspect? Everyone but her husband thinks this is natural causes. I can tell by your face you feel like you're wasting your time. Why try to freak me out? I did nothing wrong," I said.

Detective Keller stood. "I believe you. But still, as the owner of the Witch's Brew, we may need your help getting evidence or cooperation from your employees. There is another piece of evidence we're looking into that might support more than natural causes. It might be a coincidence. It might be a joke. But we must investigate as though it was serious."

"A serious what?" I asked.

"We don't disclose all of the evidence to potential witnesses or suspects. If you think of anything that was odd or might help, call us." Detective Shelley handed me her card.

"I will. I'll get Esmerelda for you if you'd like to speak to her, now," I said.

"Fine." Keller sat back down.

I subtly checked that my desk was locked as I picked up my coffee cup. Dashing downstairs, I tried to breathe.

I grabbed Esme by the arm. "Tell me you didn't have any contact with Mrs. O'Conner since she left here two days ago."

"That old bat. Why?" Esme asked.

Chapter Six

"No, no. No name calling. Promise me," I said.

"I didn't see her anywhere but here." Esme shrugged.

"You didn't run into her at a sandwich shop or a store or anywhere and argue?" I asked.

Esme frowned. "I may have gone to the library. I teach a sewing class in their extension program. The first class was yesterday afternoon, but I don't think I saw her. Is that a crime?"

"Good question. The police are in my office. She's dead, and her husband is insisting it's not natural causes. That we upset her badly that morning, and someone might've done something to her. But she was gone by yesterday, so you're okay." I rubbed my temples.

"Dead?" my aunt gasped.

"Serves the old bat right. Threatening witches," Ryan scoffed.

"What do you know about it?" I asked.

"Nothing but what I overheard. She was griping pretty loud. Over a wrong order. Really? There are bigger problems in the world." He grabbed his glass and drank some water.

"Guess his fever is better," I said to my aunt.

"His fever broke overnight. But he's still very weak." She covered him with a blanket. "Acting like a little jerk to compensate."

Pick Your Potion

"Damn, aren't there any wizards in your coven? Seriously, I could use a guy around." Ryan fluffed and punched his pillow.

"I'll send my uncle down later. Get some sleep and be quiet," I said.

"Dead?" Esme leaned again the stone wall.

"Her health was frail. You could see it in her aura. She tried hard to keep it balanced, but the littlest thing could've set off her heart or her head." Aunt Mandy tidied up.

"Head?" Esme asked.

"A stroke. Either felt like they were possible if she pushed her body too hard," Aunt Mandy said.

"She was a brittle Type 1 diabetic. But unless we goofed and put in too much or too little sweetener, I don't see how we'd be on the hook for it. Plus, she'd be testing her blood and taking insulin accordingly," I replied.

"She was pissed. Blood pressure up. But that's not something we can be charged with," Esme said.

"They want to talk to you. Since you were there and part of the spill," I said to Esme.

"I'll go, too," Aunt Mandy offered.

"No, they only wanted people who had contact with Mrs. O'Conner that morning. And if they do want to talk to you, you were down here checking on inventory. Don't mention auras or our guest down here. I'm already getting witch questions. Do we get protestors and who makes threats about it." I rubbed the back of my neck.

"Mrs. O'Conner made a threat, but she's all bluster." Esme waved it off. "I'll tell them."

54

"Tell them just what they need. Don't offer anything. Don't embellish," I said.

She turned and glared at me.

"Sorry, sometimes, I forget you're a century older than me. But you sometimes talk too much." I smiled.

Esme nodded. She was used to having power and respect in the paranormal world. She dealt with humans in specific ways. I didn't want her pushing too much with the police.

Esme headed upstairs, and I helped my aunt collect the trash. We took it upstairs and straight out the back to the alley. It was blowing snow, but we tossed the stuff in the dumpster and hustled back inside.

"Are you okay?" she asked.

"I can't believe Mrs. O'Conner is dead. I can't believe there is reason to believe we did anything bad to her." I went into the employee-only kitchen area and brewed myself some tea.

"They're just doing their job. I'm sure it's nothing. Unless you think it's an excuse to nose around here? That they're looking for Ryan?" she asked in a hushed voice.

I shook my head. "At first, I thought that. But they seem like it's routine. There is something they're not telling me. But it was all about Mrs. O'Conner. They haven't asked anything about you or Vinny. Nothing about a stranger hanging around. Nothing like that."

"Let's hope they do the autopsy and tox screen and find nothing but natural causes. We can get this off our minds. We don't need cops

Pick Your Potion

roaming around with Mr. Personality down there." I sighed then sipped my tea.

"I'll call Vin and let him know," she said.

"No, wait until they're gone. I don't want anyone acting oddly. We need to be business as usual," I said.

"The staff needs to know," she said.

"When the cops leave. They'll be asking what they wanted, anyway. But I'd rather the cops not be here with all the random questions. We've got some vampires out there. It's not the same team that was working." I fished my lip gloss out of my pocket and reapplied it.

My aunt patted my shoulder. The gloss was a nervous habit when I could do nothing. Then again, it was a very frigid winter, and my lips felt chapped.

I texted the baristas who were on that morning with Mrs. O'Conner to come in for a two o'clock meeting. Lunch could get a little busy, too, but there was a lull until the evening rush, and the evening brought in various groups and loners. I wanted as few people around as possible so it wouldn't interrupt business.

Twenty minutes later, Esme walked out of my office and escorted the detectives to the door. I was relieved when she didn't go with them.

She walked over to me at my usual table in the back corner by the kitchen. No customers wanted that table so it was my open office area. My aunt had found a project restocking the tea bags. We carried so many varieties that the baristas got overwhelmed trying to restock them during breaks, so when she needed to escape reality, she got lost in tea.

"Everything okay?" I asked Esme.

She nodded. "They want to talk to me, again. They recorded my voice."

I frowned. "Your voice? What a headache. I'm sorry she's gone, but what could we have done?"

Esme shook her head. "Nothing. Don't stress about it. They're doing their job. They'll make a fuss to impress the family. The autopsy and tests will show she died of natural causes, and it'll be over. It might take a few weeks, but they can't prove we did something that we didn't do."

I nodded. "I'm pretty sure that's what the witches from the 1600s said, too. We didn't ruin their crops so they can't prove we did."

"Stop making good points. Ignore the humans. Let them spin their wheels. She was too old and ill. It had to be natural. Who'd want to kill her?" Esme asked.

"I don't know. Maybe we should start checking into her life? Just in case," I said.

"Stay out of it," Esme warned. "But I did predict we'd never see her, again. Sometimes, my powers are wicked weird."

I laughed. "Talk about a bad way to have a right prediction."

"Now, let's talk about how to break this to the staff. Because your vamps will bolt," she said.

On the second floor, my aunt had lit a white candle and placed it at the center of the table. She burned sage just in case Mrs. O'Conner was haunting us with any negativity.

Pick Your Potion

She chanted for the soul of our dead customer as the baristas assembled for the afternoon meeting.

When we were all there, I grabbed my aunt's hand. "Would you go watch the shop? You weren't there when Mrs. O'Conner was."

"But her spirit might need help," aunt said.

"You can chant or help her reincarnate down there until a customer comes in. It'll only be a few minutes," I said.

She nodded and grabbed another white tea light candle. We put some on the bigger tables in the evenings for a little mood lighting, but I wasn't a fan of open flames. I had all the proper insurance, but customers could be careless. Enough witches had burned; I wouldn't be one of them.

"The twins are going to put together a gift basket for the family," Aunt Mandy said as she slipped out the door.

"People usually send flowers," replied Margaret, the middle-aged barista who'd made Mrs. O'Conner's drinks.

"We'll do that as well when we know when the funeral is. It seems you've all heard Mrs. O'Conner is dead. She didn't wake up yesterday morning. I don't have all the details, but apparently, she'd told her husband about her incident here and that she was really unhappy. The police think it's natural causes, *but* they have some sort of information that has them investigating until they get results back from the medical examiner."

"They came in?" asked Margaret.

"Yes, this morning. They spoke to me and Esmerelda. I had to give them all of your names, so they will likely be contacting you individually. Just tell the truth. We goofed an order. We made it right. We had a spill. We offered dry cleaning costs and free coffee."

"For a month. Too generous," Esme said.

"I'd rather be too generous than not. The point is that's all we know. I didn't see her afterward. I'm very sorry she's gone, but we didn't do anything to harm her health. She did have health issues, and odds are it will be ruled natural causes. Soon, we'll be done with the police part." I looked around. "Questions?"

"She threatened us because we're witches," said one of the younger female baristas who was also in the coven.

"She didn't do anything with it. She was just mad. A lot of people take that easy shot. Like we should magically brew things. Snap our fingers or wiggle our nose like *Bewitched,* and their coffee should be ready in seconds. We hear those comments all the time when someone has to wait. Don't look for trouble. Answer their questions, don't embellish or offer random comments. They have enough to do," I said.

"I can't believe they're investigating us for this. There are real crimes out there." Margaret sniffled back some tears.

"You did nothing wrong. None of us did. It's a shame, but she was a brittle diabetic. She had a lot of complicated medical issues. She was a balancing act. We did everything we could to

Pick Your Potion

make her happy. She didn't appear weak or ill, at all."

"I'm just nervous," Margaret admitted.

"That's okay. The police are used to people being nervous. Just admit you've never been questioned or anything before, so you're nervous. And you always have a right to have a lawyer with you if you want one." I pointed at them.

"That won't make you look guilty," Esme said.

"It's your right. It's not something they can use against you in a court," I replied.

Esme shrugged. "This is all worst-case scenarios. They're just doing their jobs. Do your jobs, answer their questions, and don't overreact."

"Any questions?" I asked

They shook their heads.

"Great. Thanks for coming in. Don't worry. Sorry for calling you in on your days off, but the police will be contacting you. Feel free to come in or call me anytime if you're worried," I said.

"Thanks," Margaret said.

"We're with you. Margaret made that drink right. Iced or hot was the only difference," said Ellen, the Wiccan barista.

"Thanks." Margaret nodded.

"We're all in this together. We might get a little bad press or a few protesters. Handle that the same way we always do, only be even nicer. More patient because someone is dead. We just want her family to have peace knowing that it was natural. Now, go on with your days. Don't let death consume your thoughts," I said.

My aunt was a hippie more than a Wiccan. She'd chant and hope for Mrs. O'Conner's reincarnation. I just hoped she found peace in the afterlife.

As the group wandered back to their day, I went downstairs. My aunt was working the counter as the twins filled a big basket with the basics.

Esme walked up. "Her husband is accusing us murder, and you're doing a gift basket?"

I picked out darker roast coffees and black teas, plus a few samplers. "We can send it to her daughter. I know she mentioned a daughter and a grandson. The hubby will get the flowers at the funeral."

"It's a nice gesture," Iris added.

"It is. I'll write a note and take it over there. Esme, I want to talk to you about the library thing. And what the cops wanted to know." I didn't want to seem bossy, but I needed to know all the information.

"Can we help?" Violet asked.

"See if you can research Mrs. O'Conner's whereabouts without bugging her family or the cops. Social media, maybe. I don't know if she used it much. I'd like to retrace her steps, if we're on the suspect list—who else is?" I was tech savvy, but the twins, who lacked magical powers, made up for it with tech skills. Violet was studying computer programming or something.

"No problem," Violet said.

"Come on, Esme," I said.

"I feel sick," she replied.

"I'll make you some healing tea. All the death talk and inquisition is hard on the spirit," Aunt Mandy said.

Pick Your Potion

"I could use some of that, please. We'll be in my office," I said.

"We did nothing wrong," Esme said as we walked.

"I know. But being in the crosshairs is stressful, and we don't know all the evidence they have. Maybe a certain stealthy black cat could sneak in there?" I asked.

"Into a police station? I'll end up in the pound." She laughed.

"True. We can't risk exposure of our actual magical powers. But we have to do something," I said.

"Agreed. Getting rid of that hunter is job number one," she said.

Chapter Seven

After a night of tossing and turning I had to agree with Esmeralda. Having Ryan here with cops sniffing around was asking for trouble. With any luck, the police thing would be over with a few tests, but I had no control over any of that. I couldn't just sit around the café waiting for the cops to come back or call. There was a business to run. I hit the bank for our weekly deposit and change. Then, I stopped a fast food place for some breakfast sandwiches and hash browns.

I dodged questions and concerns with confidence. There was only one place to get some answers, now. With a drink holder full of beverages, the food, and my inventory list, I went down to our visitor. He grumbled and hid under the blanket when he saw it was me.

"I have food, and I'm doing inventory. You can relax." I tossed a bag on him and set the coffees on the table. I pulled up a chair and ate, taking my preferred drink, just in case he thought I was trying to butter him up. I wasn't. He needed to eat, and I needed to do inventory. But info would be good.

"I knew you couldn't resist me," he said after a gulp of coffee.

"Resist, I can. Inventory must be done, and poor Aunt Mandy and Esmeralda have been down here enough. You sound like you're feeling better." I finished my food then wiped my fingers

Pick Your Potion

with a napkin. Another slug of coffee, and I was ready to get busy.

"You really hate having me here?" he asked.

"I have enough trouble with customers and the coven. I understand what happened to you, but the bravado. The flirting. The act. I can see through it. You're afraid. What are you afraid of?" I asked.

"Prison isn't enough? A charge for murder that I'm not guilty of? I mean, it was protecting innocent people and self-defense," he said.

"They obviously won't see it that way or you wouldn't be running." I pulled out my inventory tally from last month. It wasn't just a cover; I needed to do the job. I hated it and usually pawned it off on the cousins, but not this time.

He unwrapped his sandwich and sighed heavily. "The video shows me shooting the creature as it ran from me. That doesn't say self-defense but letting a werewolf loose in a mall?"

"I know. I understand that part. You can always argue he said he had a bomb, and you were defending the public."

"He didn't have a bomb. He had friends who will accuse me of murder and not stop," he said.

"Friends?" I turned and watched as he ate.

Ryan nodded and took a bite of a hash brown.

"Werewolf friends?" I asked.

"I didn't know. I thought they might be. The moon was just rising." He kept eating.

"So, these friends saw the guy shift into a werewolf? Why would they want you charged with murder if they saw the truth?" I asked.

"Maybe they knew and thought he was tame. Maybe they just want revenge. Maybe they were vampires or witches or some types that thought werewolves deserve to live and hunt because it's their nature. I don't know. But between the video and the witnesses, I can't just go home. I want to, but I'd put my hunter buddies in danger." He crumpled his trash and shot it at the garbage can.

"What about family?" I asked.

"Hunters aren't supposed to have family," he said.

"My uncle does. And everyone has *family* family. Like siblings and parents."

"Except you," he replied.

"Touché. But I had parents. They're just dead. What about you? It's not fair you know so much about me," I said.

He grinned like he was getting somewhere with all his flirting. "You've seen nearly every inch of me. I can't say that."

"And you won't. Come on. Siblings?" I asked.

"A younger sister. I won't have her visiting me in jail for doing my job." His face got hard, as though resolved to keep her good opinion of him intact.

"That's sweet. Does she know what you do for a living?" I listed a new first aid kit on my list of odds and ends. Then, I wrote a number two next to it. The hunter had really tapped us out of gauze and other supplies. They weren't used often, not since my uncle had semi-retired, but they were necessary.

Pick Your Potion

"No, not really. She thinks I'm a bounty hunter. It explains the lifestyle and the guns." He shrugged.

"I like that. Makes sense while you go after fugitive werewolves or vampires," I replied.

"I left her a message that I'm on a hunt for a motorcycle gang that attacked a young woman. They skipped bail and went on the road together, so some hunters and I teamed up to protect people. We'll split the bonds." He sat up a little straighter.

"Nice story. You should write books," I teased him.

"You get good at thinking fast and fibbing to protect others. I have to keep her safe," he said.

"What happened to your parents?" I asked.

"My dad bailed when I was little. He went out for a drink with his buddies and never came home. Mom worked herself to death at unskilled jobs. I mowed lawns and washed cars until I was old enough to deliver pizzas. That's how I discovered the other world." He looked at me like I was part of it.

Was I the enemy in his eyes?

"You discovered werewolves delivering pizza?" I asked.

He grinned and nodded. "I worked late. As late as I could. This one place delivered to a college, and they stayed open twenty-four hours. I took the shift after dinner, so I did my homework, had dinner with my sister, and then went to work until the sun came up. The owner warned me to never approach anything that looked like a stray dog. They gave me pepper spray for the dogs. And a wooden stake. There were jokes about Buffy and Lestat. I thought it was a hazing joke for the new kid."

"Until..." I prompted.

"Until I delivered a bunch of pizzas to a frat house. There were two delivery guys—that's how many pizzas they ordered. So, I wasn't alone, at least. They opened the door, and it was a bloody mess. People screaming. Trying to run."

"The vampires opened the door? You'd think they'd have enough to feed on," I said.

"They did, but they wanted more. They had some people tied up, untouched. Later, I found that the vamps were saving those. They were virgin blood. Luckily, I didn't have that problem. I dropped my pizzas and ran. Like a fool." He laughed.

"They caught you," I filled in.

"Of course. The other delivery guy, Jack, he had a stake in his pocket at least. He killed a couple before they fed on him. He had bite marks all over his body."

"And you?" I asked.

"I ran, but there wasn't a point. Vamps move quicker than you can blink, and more and more just kept coming. There are some really bad groups called nests that hunt together. They ended up dragging me back in the house. I fought them off and ran, trying to escape. They enjoyed watching me run in a panic, circling through the house like a cornered rat. A female tried a different approach—offered whatever I wanted if she could feed. I was tempted but got lucky. I ended up in a room where some kid had been

Pick Your Potion

doing pot. I grabbed his lighter and torched the ugly curtains. It set off the sprinklers, but I shouted fire. Vampires can't fight fire." He rolled on his back and folded his arms under his head. "They took off while it was still dark. I called for ambulances and stuff. Untied people and helped. I couldn't help Jack." He sighed.

"That's very heroic. I don't know if I'd have been that brave at sixteen," I admitted.

"You would've been. Tough witch like you."

I rolled my eyes at him. "That's how found out about vampires and werewolves. How did you get into hunting? It's a pretty tight network."

"Sure. Well, my boss heard about it, and he was in the network. He didn't want his employees getting eaten. I got some more training and met some guys. They did construction and went hunting at night. Come to think of it, they might've been gypsies, but no one ever talked about anything but the hunt. It was like families and other stuff didn't exist."

Something didn't add up. "How did that help your family? I mean, hunting doesn't pay."

"That was the problem. I dropped out of high school and worked construction during the day. The guys just fudged my age. Then, at night, I could hunt, keep my mom and sister safe from those things, and we had plenty of money from my day job."

"When did you sleep?" I asked.

"I had days off from both. If you scheduled it right, the job was covered, the hunting was covered, and everyone got just enough rest." He shrugged. "I miss that."

"I'm sure your sister appreciated the effort. Now, she can take care of herself," I said.

"She's a nurse, so she does fine. I just miss my crew and my friends. I don't know when it'll be safe to go back," he said.

"Never. The statute of limitations doesn't expire on murder. You might want to pick a new home and start over," I suggested.

"They're probably bugging my sister nonstop about where I am. If I've been in contact with her. I want to go back and protect her." He kicked at the blankets.

"She's better off without you there, and you know it. I'm sure your hunter friends got her a message safely. If you resettle somewhere, she can always relocate to join you." It was sweet that he loved his sister, but she didn't need to be tangled up in his world.

"She might be getting married. I want her to have a normal life. Your uncle had a family and hunted. Was that weird?" he asked.

"He worked in a gypsy family business and hunted with his brothers. We had enough money. Aunt Mandy taught classes in yoga and meditation. She cleaned people's auras and helped them balance. She worked out of the house, so she was always there but brought in good money. It was a happy childhood," I said.

"Do you remember your parents?" he asked.

When had this gone from getting more info about his case to sharing childhood crap? I shook my head. "That's not relevant."

"Relevant to what? We're just talking," he said.

Pick Your Potion

"I want to know if there is anything you're hiding. Anything I don't know. Because we have police around, now." My history had nothing to do with the present problems.

"Mrs. O'Conner's my fault? She was sick, and her number came up. Don't blame me," he said.

"I'm not blaming you. I have cops asking questions. If they want to search the place and find you, I'm on the hook for harboring a fugitive. Is there somewhere we can move you to? Cousins? Friends? Not back home, farther away. They could be tracking you. I want you to be safe, but I want my family to be safe, as well," I admitted.

"And I thought you were one of us. Brave and willing to risk your life for the right things," he shot back.

"Claudia," Uncle Vinny said.

I hadn't heard him come down the stairs.

"Have you heard?" I asked him.

"About the customer, yes. We need to talk," he said.

"Follow me. I have to do inventory." I headed for the stockroom, deeper in the basement maze.

I started ticking off the things that needed reordering.

"It's not Ryan's fault," Vinny said.

"I know. But it adds risk. Risk for him because the cops are around. If we can move him, we should. They could be tracking him down. He's been here long enough." I wanted to protect my café and people, but Ryan would be safer not staying here.

"You think the cops aren't watching this place, just in case? Moving him now would raise suspicions and questions," Vinny said.

I sighed and kept working. "I understand. We have to be careful. Why is this all happening at once?"

He put his hand on my shoulder. "We'll make it through this. I know dealing with a human death is bringing a lot of scary attention. But this could happen to any shop. They're just doing their job. You need to simply be helpful, answer the questions, and don't offer anything beyond what they want. Don't act like you have anything to hide. Ryan is doing better, but he could open up those wounds easily if he had to run. Then, he reinfects his wounds. With the cops around, we're not moving him."

He used that fatherly tone. Even though he wasn't my father, he was the only father figure I'd had growing up. He was always there for me. Protected me and treated me like I was his. My instinct said to trust his advice. I hadn't even considered the cops could be watching us.

"You're right. We don't want to draw attention to ourselves. But I think the cops believe it's natural causes. They just need the medical proof. The family is pushing for the investigation, and I can't blame them, but we didn't do anything to her. I understand they want someone to blame, but if she asked for a sugary drink, what? We're not supposed to give it to her? We were supposed to know she was a brittle diabetic?" I was paranoid enough about peanuts and other allergies.

Pick Your Potion

"No, of course not. You give them what they ask for. She had the responsibility to manage her own health and all that sugar testing stuff. Getting stressed out or spiking her blood pressure doesn't mean Esme or you gave her a heart attack later that day. That's just crazy. Grieving people want someone to blame, but the law won't fall for that. You've got nothing to worry about," he said.

"The cops seemed to indicate they had some reason to be chatting with us first. They took a sample of Esme's voice. The cops will be back." I sighed.

"Did you send over the gift basket the twins made?" he asked.

I shook my head. "I wasn't sure if it might look like we were trying too hard. If her husband is accusing us and we take him something, it'll probably only make it worse. I could try with his daughter, but I don't want to look like we're trying to smooth something over."

"You'll know when the time is right. Finish the inventory and try to have a normal day," he said.

"Fine. You spend some time with Ryan. He's complaining there are no men around here," I said.

"You like hiring vampires instead of human men," Vinny teased.

"They're more loyal and do what they're told. I have some human guys. But they're here to work, not entertain a guy hiding out." I shrugged.

"I'll take care of it. Back to work," he said.

Once he left to chat with Ryan, I used my magic to levitate the items that needed to be

72

reordered, filling out the list as I noted the supplies that hovered above the rest. Then, I cast another spell for anything we'd need seasonally to show itself. The heart stuff popped up. Ah yes, next month was Valentine's Day. I added seasonal goodies and cups. Love made people splurge, and we'd sell a lot of ceramic mug sets.

Right now, I'd just love to have Ryan safely moved on and Mrs. O'Conner's case closed. Romance was the furthest thing from my mind.

Pick Your Potion

Chapter Eight

That afternoon, I forced myself to stop checking the Internet and local news feeds. There was no story or mention of us anywhere. There was also no obituary yet for Mrs. O'Conner. I set alerts on both so I didn't become obsessed with checking things. Aunt Mandy and Esme were business as usual. I didn't know how they could be so calm.

I sat in my office, placing the orders, so we were stocked for the coming weeks based on prior use. Part of me worried that bad press could hurt sales. but I wanted to stay positive. We'd done nothing wrong. and any concerns would blow over.

A sharp knock on the door made me jump. "Come in," I said.

Margaret walked in. "There is an older man outside the shop telling people not to come in."

"Mr. O'Conner?" I asked, but I didn't need an answer.

"We assume so, but he wasn't a customer. We don't know him. No one has spoken to him yet," she replied.

"I will. Get me a large black coffee." I grabbed my jacket.

January could be brutally cold in the Northeast. I had my North Face jacket and stretchy gloves on and walked out front by the time Margaret had the coffee ready.

Pick Your Potion

Before leaving the café, I studied the widower. The man was in his late sixties and looked flustered. I couldn't blame him, but this wasn't going to bring her back.

I walked out in the bracing cold and offered him the coffee.

"Mr. O'Conner, can I help you?" I asked.

"You did this. Your shop," he said.

"I'm Claudia, and this is my shop. I know you're upset. I was very sorry to hear about your wife. I promise you we did nothing to hurt her." I held out the coffee, again, but he ignored it.

"Liar. You upset her. She was never coming back here." He pointed to the shop.

"I know. She told us. We did everything we could to make it up to her. If she didn't want to come back, fine. One spill or a wrong order didn't kill her. She never drank the iced coffee. The only thing she drank was what she ordered. Why don't you come inside and we can talk about this in private?" I was getting cold, even in my fuzzy boots.

He glared at me. "Fine. It's freezing out here today."

I led the way and settled behind my desk, rubbing my hands together. He sat across from me and sipped the coffee.

"I understand you're upset that your wife had a bad experience here. But if she was in any way sick or unsteady on her feet, we would've called for an ambulance. We don't want to lose a customer, but when she left, she was fine. There are plenty of people who can verify that. I'm sure the police will be talking to them. They already talked to me. I'm sure you know that," I said.

He nodded. "They're not done looking into things."

"Then, why protest outside of my shop? Let the police do their job first. Your wife was a customer here for years. One bad day doesn't mean we're evil. I think she'd have come back to us after a few weeks of those chain coffee shops." I nodded.

"She hated the chains. But she was so mad at this place." He shook his head. "Even if the police can't prove anything, I know it was your fault. Maybe legally I can't prove it, but this place upset her. She had a weak heart, and too much stress wasn't good for her."

"We offered a month of free coffee. What more could we do? People make mistakes. I'm sure working at the library had its stresses, too. You want to dump it all on me?" I asked.

"Someone has to pay. I shouldn't be talking to you," he said.

He put the cup on my desk and hefted himself to his feet.

"Why?" I asked.

"There is an ongoing investigation. They told me not to. I believe you didn't mean to kill her. But you are responsible for what happens here. You're awfully young to own a place like this," he said.

I nodded. Maybe I shouldn't be talking to him either. I didn't want to cause more suspicion for myself or the café with the police.

Pick Your Potion

"Maybe you should leave, then. Or I could call the police and let them know you're protesting here," I said.

"I can be outside. They said not to go in or talk to you. You're right; I should leave. But you'll be dealing with my protest plenty." He stormed out.

I followed him and watched him take up the same spot.

Aunt Mandy walked over to me. "What did he say?"

"Nothing new. He said he's not supposed to talk to me. I tried to calm him down and assure him that we would've called for help if we thought she was ill. I don't think he's reasonable, now. He's stuck in his grief." I wished I knew a way to help him, not that he'd listen to me.

"I can try to help him," she offered.

"No, I know you can help, but he won't listen. He's not ready, and coming from us, it'll only make him dig in his heels more." I leaned on the counter.

"What should we do? He'll freeze out there," Margaret said.

"Give him half an hour. If he's still there, let me know," I said.

"Half an hour?" My aunt followed me up the second floor where I wanted some peace and quiet.

"He's got a big coat and gloves on. I'm not parenting my customers or my protesters. If he's still there, I'll call that Detective Shelley who left her card, so she can come and talk to him. If we just call the cops, it'll turn into a mess." I flopped down in an overstuffed chair.

One of the cats jumped in my lap and started purring. I needed the feline therapy.

"I meditated on this last night. We must not bury our heads in the sand and hide." My aunt took a brush to the other cat who flipped and rolled for more attention.

"I talked to Uncle Vinny. He said we can't move Ryan. The police might be watching us for anything unusual. I think we should act normal and not meddle." I scratched my feline friend under the chin until she shook her head.

"I understand that. But you can deliver that gift basket and speak to the O'Conners' daughter. Maybe she can diffuse the situation. The twins have tracked down some of Mrs. O'Conner's day, but more details from the daughter might help. And you can feel her out to see if she feels like her father or is more reasonable. If you did nothing wrong, you have nothing to be ashamed of or fear," she said.

"But we're witches, and I don't know about drawing attention to ourselves." I looped my fingers with the cat's tail until she turned around and head butted me.

"Esmeralda insists we ignore this and stay out of it as much as possible. Let the humans sort out what happened. I agree, but that doesn't mean we should be rude. She was a regular customer. A condolence gift basket is appropriate. I can take it over, if you prefer," my aunt offered.

That made me feel queasy. She was sweet and would never get us into trouble, but my aunt didn't know how not to get involved. She couldn't help herself. My aunt cared too much about

Pick Your Potion

everyone. People could take advantage of her because she'd trust them and help them. My uncle and I protected her from being taken in.

"No, thanks. I don't want to put anyone in the middle. I'll handle it. Tomorrow. I can't think about it today," I said.

"You were down there talking to Ryan for a while. Everything okay?" she asked with a smile.

"Fine. We talked a bit about things. I wanted to try and find out if there was more to his story. He told me about his family and sister. He changed the subject, sort of, and I didn't want to start a fight." I shrugged.

"Men. Vin won't tell me the details of Ryan's case more than what you know. He said it's all hearsay because the police and mall witnesses don't know what they were really looking at. They don't know a werewolf or a vampire from a human. Things happen fast, and they see what they believe. Their brain makes sense of what doesn't make sense. But if Ryan didn't want to share, that's unfortunate."

"He's not my permanent problem. Once this is over, we can move him on. He can start over somewhere else. I can't let it hurt the café or the coven." I scratched the cat's ears.

"You truly believe Mrs. O'Conner died of natural causes?" Aunt Mandy asked.

I'd never questioned it. "That's the feeling I got from the police. Her age and health. If someone did harm her, it wasn't us," I said.

Aunt Mandy nodded. "I agree, but nothing is for sure, yet."

I stood and went down the stairs enough to see Margaret.

She shrugged. "He's still there," she said.

I took out my phone and called the detective. I didn't want to get the old guy in trouble, but I wasn't going to have him die of frostbite or catch pneumonia from being stubborn.

"You're sure?" my aunt asked.

"We don't need more bad publicity. He's bringing enough. If he gets sick or dies from exposure, I don't want that on my conscience," I said.

"Detective Shelley," the cop answered.

Pick Your Potion

Chapter Nine

I felt so human. Standing on the porch of Dana Stevens' Cape Cod-style home, I was tempted to use magic to get me out of this problem. Dana was Mrs. O'Conner's daughter, and I had the gift basket. That wasn't the worst part. Mr. O'Conner protesting outside of my café in the bitter cold was the problem. The police had talked him home the other day, but he was back there this morning.

I rang the doorbell as I made up a spell in my head. I could cast one on Mr. O'Conner to remove his anger or need for revenge. But the world had to have balance, so that anger would transfer somewhere else where it wasn't deserved or didn't belong. It'd be my fault. That would be a bad spell.

A woman about forty years old answered the door. "Can I help you?"

"Hi, I don't know if you have a minute to talk. I'm Claudia Crestwood, owner of Witch's Brew. I wanted to bring you this and tell you how sorry I am for your loss. We miss your mother's daily visits." I held out the basket in front of me, just in case she had some anger like her father.

"I'm not sure you should be here," she said.

I frowned. "I'm not trying to cause trouble. I just wanted to talk to you. Your father is very upset, and I can't seem to have a conversation with him. He's going to get himself sick standing

Pick Your Potion

out in the cold, protesting my shop, and I don't want that any more than you do."

"Come inside," she said.

We sat in a comfortable kitchen with white and blue checkered chair cushions, towels, and accents. It felt very country and sweet.

"I'm very sorry about your mother, but if we had any idea she was ill, we'd have called for help. She was fine when she left," I said.

Dana held up a hand. "That's not the issue."

"It's not?" I asked.

She set down two cups of coffee. "My mother had health issues. Her doctor believes it was natural. She went about her normal day, and there were plenty of people after you that spiked her blood pressure more than your little shop."

"I'm glad you understand. Your father is protesting outside the shop, and it's hurting my business. I know that's nothing compared to what you're going through, but it's not safe for him. The bitter cold and his age. We'll keep calling the police for well checks on him," I said.

"I told him that's crazy. He'll give himself a heart attack. But he's convinced someone did something to Mom. Her health was stable. She'd been diabetic most of her life, so she knew how to manage that. I think it must've been her heart or something just changed. But my father won't consider that. He wanted to grow old with her." She sipped her coffee.

"I understand. He's convinced someone hurt her. We were her first stop, and he probably heard her complain about us. Is there any way you could talk to him and make him understand?" I asked.

84

She smiled. "I've tried. He knows she can be harsh and irritate people. But she's worked at the library for years and been part of the garden club forever. She's had the same friends all her life. Fights and getting over the fights. Ups and downs. You're the new thing. Your shop is only a few years old. She liked the old diner that was there previously. She hated the coffee chains more than your café, but she did like trying all the different stuff without it being as pretentious."

"So, your father can't blame her co-workers, friends, garden club, and so on. He probably is friends with the husbands of the garden club members. And friends' husbands."

"They did a lot of couple things. And he likes going to the library. So, in his mind, it can't be anyone there. Even though she's made her share of enemies everywhere. I know she could be hard to please." Dana rubbed her forehead.

"I'm sorry; I'm not making this easier on you. I just wanted you to know that no one at our shop had any grudges against your mother. She tried all sorts of drinks, and the baristas liked that. They get bored with the same things every day. She had high standards, but that kept my people on their toes. She never said our place wasn't clean or stocked. That made me feel good." I shrugged.

"She was very hard to please. I wish they'd just do those tests and we could know. I know there is a backup. Life in a city. The morgue and medical examiner's office are understaffed, I guess. But that's the only thing my father will listen to. Someone in authority saying it was her

Pick Your Potion

heart or a stroke. Or someone else confessing they did something bad." She frowned.

"Was there any enemy she especially had a problem with lately?" I asked.

Dana shook her head. "Most of the stuff is old. History that bubbles up when they disagree. But, really, I shouldn't be talking to you while the investigation is still open."

She stood, and I did, as well.

"Your father said the same thing, I don't understand why. I think you believe me that we didn't do anything to harm her," I said.

"There were some threats made. The police are investigating. I don't know who did it or why, but it's hard to ignore. It's scary to hear them. I think you should go," she said.

"Threats against you?" I asked.

She stared at me.

"Against your mother since she died?" I asked.

"I'm not supposed to talk to you or anyone about them," she said.

"Why would you let me in your house if you thought I had anything to do with it?" I pressed.

She walked to the front door and opened it. "I wanted to hear your voice. See if it felt familiar."

"Does it?" I asked as I approached the door.

"Please just go. I'll speak to my father about risking his health outside in this cold. My mother wouldn't want that. My son only has one grandparent left." She was near tears. This really hadn't gone as planned.

"I'm sorry to hear that." I stepped out onto the porch. "I won't bother you, anymore. Please just know that no one hurt her at my café. And I certainly didn't threaten anyone, just for the record."

She closed the door in my face.

I climbed into my little green VW Bug and warmed up. That hadn't gone at all like I'd hoped. But at least she didn't believe we'd hurt her mother. There was a logical reason her father blamed us—anyone else would mean blaming a friend, and he couldn't bring himself to do that.

But threats against Mrs. O'Conner? The voice sample from Esme made sense, now. Her voice was deeper with a bit of raspiness to it. Mine was much higher. Maybe I didn't sound like whoever had threatened them. Wouldn't they disguise their voice? I texted Detective Shelley that I needed more information. Trying to smooth things over might be making things worse, somehow.

Sipping hot tea, I sat at the back table in the café and waited for the detective. Mr. O'Conner was still blustering outside to keep people out. Fred from the sandwich shop next door had tried to convince Mr. O'Conner to go home or at least have some soup. The old man was stubborn. Detective Shelley walked up to the door, and they exchanged a few words.

Mr. O'Conner finally packed up and got into his car.

The detective came in and headed right for my table.

"Is that why you wanted to see me?" she asked and nodded toward Mr. O'Conner.

Pick Your Potion

"No, but thank you. The other shop owners have tried to talk sense into him or warm him up, but he doesn't listen to anyone." I gestured to the chair opposite me.

"Want something to drink?" Ellen, one of our baristas, asked.

"Large hot coffee, regular," she said.

"Refill, please. Thanks," I said.

"What was so urgent?" Shelley asked.

"I tried to speak to Mr. O'Conner yesterday. He started talking but then said he shouldn't be here, and we shouldn't be talking. It seemed odd. Today, I went to see his daughter. Just to deliver a gift basket for condolence and talk about her father's protest. His safety."

"It's interfering with your business," she said.

Ellen dropped off the drinks.

"Thanks, Ellen." I nodded and took a sip.

"Yes, fine. Mr. O'Conner is hurting my business and the other businesses in the area. I can handle it. Mrs. Stevens seems sure it was natural causes and her father is just grieving. But then, she said we shouldn't be talking either. She mentioned threats. You took a voice sample from Esmeralda. I need to know the whole story," I said.

"The investigation is ongoing, but we've gotten far enough along. There were threats against Mrs. O'Conner after she'd made her insults to your shop and witches. Her husband got a phone call at home. The voice sounded female but also distorted. He let the machine get the rest of the calls that afternoon. It wasn't Esmeralda, and no one thinks it's you. There was a note left in the mailbox, as well. That's part of why we can't dismiss the idea that someone did do something to Mrs. O'Conner. Without the threats before her sudden death, there would be much less reason to put people on the case." She was choosing her words very carefully.

"I understand. She did threaten our witch theme and pagan ways. But more than a few people have made rude remarks. Especially if they don't know the history of the city. Salem gets all the attention for the witch trials. It's part of the history here, too, and brings in some tourists. People lash out when they're having a bad day. I don't take it personally." I rolled my eyes.

"Thank you for confirming that Mrs. O'Conner mentioned something about you being witches. I don't believe you mentioned that, at first," she said.

I shrugged. "It didn't seem relevant. No one has ever done anything more than a little protesting. We decorate for Christmas and Easter, as well as all the other major holidays. We're not trying convert anyone."

"But someone took offense to her threats and made ones of their own. Were members of your coven here?" she asked.

"Esmeralda. My aunt, but she couldn't threaten a mouse in her kitchen. There might've been some customers. A couple of the staff are. I can give you a list, but I hate the idea of my coven being harassed. I can be sure of the staff that was here but not of all the customers. Plus, word travels." I couldn't believe someone would threaten a customer.

Pick Your Potion

"I understand. But it means someone heard about her threats and had a problem with her enough to make their own threats, and the woman was found dead the next day. You see, we have to investigate until the medical examiner comes back with cause of death. We did ask the family to keep their distance and not talk to you or anyone else about it. Tried to keep the threats a surprise piece of information, but Mr. O'Conner can't seem to stay away."

"He's upset. I just don't want him to get frostbite or have a heart attack. He shouts at people and gets so worked up in the cold." I shook my head. "I'm sure he loved his wife very much, but she wouldn't want him to end up in the hospital."

"Thank you for calling me yesterday. The patrol car took him home. The officer had a talk with him. I called him later on. I'm not sure there is anything we can do short of arresting him to keep him from coming back. But if he's there for more than an hour at a time, call, and we'll have a patrol car take him home," she said.

"I will, and I'll let every shift manager know, in case he tries protesting overnight. I hope he's not that crazy. What a thing for your officers to do. Our tax dollars at work. Any idea how long before we get the information from the autopsy?" I asked.

"Could be another week. The results will be accurate. They are short-staffed. And there were a lot of deaths over the holidays. More than normal need to be tested and autopsied. The tox screen should be soon."

"Odds are that'll show nothing?" I asked.

"Most likely. We talked to her family and searched her things. No sign of drugs or abusing alcohol. Someone would've had to slip her poison. But to time that so perfectly that it worked overnight? I think Mrs. O'Conner got what most of us want in a death. To go to sleep one night and just not wake up." Detective Shelley smiled.

"But she was only in her sixties. I'd like to make it to at least eighty before I didn't wake up. She didn't have cancer or any other disease that might've hastened things?" I asked.

"Being Type 1 diabetic for as long as she was, it's serious. We think of people living with diabetes all the time. So it's not a death sentence, but it weakens the body and takes a toll. Type 2 can be cured and managed easier. Type 1 is rougher. I've had quite an education from her doctor and the ME. Mrs. O'Conner had some issues medically before. Her doctor wanted her to keep active but also rest and eat healthier. So, we'll let you know when we find out about the results. And if we find out who threatened her, that would go a long way to removing suspicion from your café. If you could provide me with a list of coven members who frequent your café, that'd be helpful." She nodded.

"I'll email it to you. I just can't imagine any of them making threats to a regular customer over a bad morning. Mrs. O'Conner never would've done anything. I keep expecting her to come through the door." I sipped my tea.

"Well, now, you understand why this isn't a closed case. I wish we could clear you and all your

Pick Your Potion

friends, but the threat specified witches. So, it sorts of shines a spotlight on your establishment. Thanks for the coffee. Send me that list by tonight, please."

Chapter Ten

That night, I called a coven meeting. Technically, I had Esmeralda send the email. Everyone assembled on the second floor at ten p.m. The café was quiet but still had some customers, so we moved into my locked room.

"Did they get the results?" Ellen asked.

I sighed. "No. The autopsy could be another week or so. Hopefully, we'll hear about the toxicology screen tomorrow. That may or may not help. The reason that the investigation is focused on us and isn't just standard procedure is that someone made threats against Mrs. O'Conner the day she died."

"What?" Aunt Mandy gasped.

"Yes, after she left here but before she died. Her husband let their machine record most of them for the police. As she was leaving, Mrs. O'Conner did make some comments about us being witches and the name of the café. Well, someone called her home and made threats. Someone also left a note in the mailbox that was found the next day after she had passed away." I looked around at the stunned faces.

"So, they aren't just picking on us because we are witches?" Ellen asked.

"No, they are following evidence. Someone left those messages. They even took a voice sample from me the day they told us about Mrs.

Pick Your Potion

O'Conner. They didn't want us to know about the threats," Esmeralda said.

"Because we'd protect each other?" Iris asked.

"Probably. I want to know who threatened Mrs. O'Conner. Someone went to a lot of trouble to find her phone number. To find her address. They were at her house. I need to be sure that we don't have a snake in our midst. We don't threaten people. We don't hurt people or wish harm on them." I made eye contact with many around the room, hoping I could discern the guilty party...if they were here.

"You really think they're among us?" Esme asked.

"I don't know. We must wait out the police investigation. That means bad publicity for the café. Mr. O'Conner has been protesting outside daily. And we must hope that the medical examiner has a clear cause of death. I don't like waiting. I'm not very patient," I said.

"We know that," Violet said.

"What can we do?" Aunt Mandy asked.

"We could cast a spell on Mr. O'Conner to keep him at home," Esme suggested.

"No, we're not doing spells on innocent people unless it's absolutely necessary. That could backfire and make us look guilty, as well."

"It'd make us look like witches," someone from the crowd joked.

"Cute. But since someone did something bad in the name of witches, we should find out who. That's my first priority because I need to know I can trust my coven." I'd worked on the spell most of the afternoon. There was a family spell book in

94

the back. Most witches used standard spells, but I liked making my own.

I opened my hand and a red ball of light floated from my palm.

"What's that going to do?" asked an older witch.

"Find the guilty party. Whoever threatened Mrs. O'Conner will have the red light hover over their heads," I said.

When I pulled my hand away, the ball of light darted around the room, reading all the individuals. It zigged and zagged briefly near every woman in the room. Finally, it darted out the window.

The twins ran to the window. "It's gone," they said.

"Damn. Did you put a tracker on it?" Esme asked.

"No, I just wanted to rule out us," I replied sheepishly. I was good at spells, but sometimes, I wasn't as good at thinking things all the way through. But Esmerelda had a hundred years on me.

"Well, it wasn't anyone here. But the police won't accept a spell as proof, anyway," Ellen said.

I smiled. "True, but I feel better. I know some of you are out to defend Wicca and paganism. You want to make more of a statement. I'd understand if Mrs. O'Conner's threats upset you. We have the freedom of religion. We also have a responsibility to the paranormal creatures out there. The magical world must be protected. At least I feel like we have that obligation. If you don't, there are other covens focused on more traditional Wiccan

Pick Your Potion

things. But we don't want witch hunts, vampire hunts, or werewolf hunts. Can you imagine what big game hunters would pay to hunt a werewolf?"

"You're giving the humans all the power," Ellen said.

"No, I'm not forgetting our history," I replied.

"Then, why are you keeping a hunter in your basement? Protecting them and the werewolves is a bit of a contradiction," said one of the members.

"I understand it's hard to reconcile for some people. Some people believe vamps and weres should run wild. If they kill, it's their nature. But they are sentient beings capable of making choices, and choosing to kill is a crime. I won't tolerate it. If they kill too many humans, we'll be at war. The humans will hunt all of us down. Hunters have controlled the killing vamps and weres for centuries. It's not a perfect system, but it works. Sometimes, a hunter is caught on tape, and the police want to charge them. So, we're helping one. He was severely injured. Right now, the police are watching us, so moving the hunter is not an option. Once the case is resolved, he'll move on. You have my word—I'm not running a bed and breakfast for hunters." I rubbed the bridge of my nose as tension built behind my eyes.

"Maybe the café wasn't a great cover for this. Maybe a yoga studio?" Aunt Mandy suggested.

Esme shook her head. "Yoga is too much of a trend. You'd have to change out the main offering. Pilates is more in, now."

"Fortune telling?" Iris suggested.

"The gypsies have that market sewn up. You don't want them for enemies," I said.

"Candles and incense," Violet said.

Ellen stood. "Coffee and tea is good. We do a great business, and people talk. They talk on their phones and to their friends about anything. And we baristas listen. We know who hates Trump and who secretly supports him. Who never orders anything with the witch themes—those tend to be the strict bible thumpers who like our coffee but not the theme. Most people don't care. But we get all sorts of people in here for coffee. If you go to something more new age, you lose the people we want to keep an eye on. We need to be more Harry Potter."

"Harry Potter was protested in some areas," Esme said.

"But the vast majority of kids and parents approved. It was full of witches and werewolves but made people feel good. We can do that," Aunt Mandy said.

"A Harry Potter party?" I asked.

"Maybe for Halloween. I think we can revamp the wall by the front door. That plaque dedicated to the fallen witches in the 1600s that tells people about the history—it's good, but it might be in the wrong place," Aunt Mandy said.

"Hide the truth and put out the happy fake version?" Esme asked.

"It'd probably work. Move that plaque behind the counter. Move some of the cute witches from TV and movies around, so it's a mix." Iris nodded.

"Right. What if we made up a quiz? Which witch or wizard are you? They fill out a quiz and turn it in for a free small drink and the results." Violet pulled out her phone and made notes.

Pick Your Potion

"Sounds like an app," I said.

"Exactly. What, you thought paper?" Iris rolled her eyes at me.

"Never. So, campier funny witches. More 'Sabrina the Teenage Witch' and less Maleficent. Maybe Esme could sit on the counter in cat form and crack jokes like Salem?" I teased.

"We've veered off the goal of this meeting." She glared at me.

"You're right, we have. I'm sorry. The café is a cover for working with paranormal beings. Trying to keep the peace with humans by keeping an eye on them. Keeping them close rather than pushing them away. A little rearrangement of the pics can't hurt. I like that app idea. Maybe we have the TVs in the main lounge play *Sabrina*, *Bewitched*, the *Harry Potter* movies, and so on. *Hocus Pocus*, *Practical Magic*. There are plenty of those shows and movies out there. Get the DVDs cheap and have theme weekends. It could become a thing. I get sick of news and morning talk shows that go on all day."

"But in the morning, people are watching the weather and traffic," Ellen added.

"True. So, the TV over the baristas stays on local weather, traffic, and news during morning rush. But the rest can play. Heck, *Charmed*. Get all of Buffy and Angel. I don't want the staff to get sick of repeats. Mix it up, cute and light. Nothing too dark. We have the TVs on, but people generally ignore them." I looked around.

"This is more of a business decision. Which is good. But the coven is under suspicion by cops," a member spoke up.

98

I had skipped over that a bit. "That's true, and the police might contact you to find out where you were and what you were doing. Don't be afraid. Tell the truth. No one here did it. I trust my spell worked. But understand that we're not about attacking anyone. Any human. That's not going to help this situation or our overall goals."

"So, what do we do?" Iris asked.

"Esmeralda and I came up with another spell. We're going to find out, now, if Mrs. O'Conner's death with natural or not. Then, I'll know best how to proceed." I set out the medium-sized cauldron.

Esme filled it with core ingredients and stirred. "It'll only work if we have something that belonged to Mrs. O'Conner. What do you have?"

I smiled and pulled a little plastic bag from my pocket. "Hair from her daughter's coat. I grabbed it as I left her house."

"That'll work?" Aunt Mandy asked.

"The daughter belonged to her mother. We just have to phrase it right." I nodded to Esme.

"You can do it," Esme said.

Great, no pressure! "Life and death. Good and evil. I ask for the truth to be revealed. Was the mother of this woman taken by nature or killed by mortal hands?" I dropped the hair in the mixture.

A puff of smoke later, and the brew turned red.

Pick Your Potion

Chapter Eleven

"Red means?" Iris asked.

"Not natural," I replied.

"Green would've meant natural," Esme added.

"She was killed. We didn't do it, but she was killed by someone's actions." I leaned slightly on the table.

"Or inactions," Aunt Mandy said.

"Now what? The police won't take that as evidence. Even if they would, we don't want them to think it's us," Ellen said.

"Agreed. We keep it quiet since it means nothing to them," Violet said.

"We don't want them to take it as a confession from anyone. Whoever made those threats screwed us over, but the police aren't on a witch hunt." I sat down.

"Now, we wait?" my aunt asked.

I shook my head. "I have a list of where Mrs. O'Conner was, more or less. Work at the library and her garden club. The twins have been stalking her social media and her friends. So, I'll fill in the blanks."

"You're going to solve the murder?" Esme asked.

"Someone has to. They're looking in the wrong places or they think it's just natural causes. We know it's something more. Her daughter admitted that Mrs. O'Conner could be harsh and

Pick Your Potion

had some enemies. It's worth talking to people," I said.

My aunt frowned. "It's dangerous."

"I agree. You need to stay out of it. Let the police spin their wheels and figure it out. It's not us. It's not our problem," Esme said.

"Yeah, we can call the cops on Mr. O'Conner every time we see him. Just wait until we get the test results and the cops do whatever," Ellen said.

"So, let someone get away with murder? That's not right either," Violet said.

"It's not a paranormal crime or problem. That's what we should be involved with," Esme said.

"But this case threatens our coven and our work. If it comes back with evidence that someone hurt her, we could be first in line as suspects. I'd rather know who else might've had a grudge or a motive. I'm going to discreetly ask some questions and see what comes up. I can't do nothing. If you don't like it, tough. Meeting adjourned." I walked down the stairs.

I was at the library when it opened with a to-go carrier full of coffee. The staff was happy, and it broke the ice.

"This is a nice treat. What brings it on?" Mrs. Drew asked.

Mrs. Drew was the head librarian and skeptical. She was a bit younger than Mrs. O'Conner but not much.

"Well, Mrs. O'Conner was a regular customer. I know she worked here. I just wondered if anyone knows what really happened. She left my shop in good health, if not happy about an order mix-up," I said.

"And that spill. She was so upset. Her husband brought her a new set of clothes from home," said Audrey, a redheaded part-timer.

"Accidents happen. I just wondered if she seemed ill to anyone else or things got worse," I said.

"The police have been here," Mrs. Drew said. "We answered their questions."

"I understand. It's just been bugging me. We're waiting on test results. But Mr. O'Conner is so angry. He blames my shop, and I'm just trying to figure out why or what we can do," I replied.

A few of the women just shook their heads and went back to work.

"Maybe we should speak alone," Mrs. Drew said.

"Sure." I followed her into her office.

"If you're trying to throw suspicion onto us, it won't work," Mrs. Drew said.

"I'm not trying to throw anything. The police seem to think it was natural causes. It's Mr. O'Conner who seems to be pushing to find someone to blame. I know Mrs. O'Conner was fine when she left my shop. I'm just trying to narrow down when she started to show signs of illness or whatever I can find out," I replied.

"I've known the O'Conners for a long time. If there is reason to think something else happened, I'm sure Mr. O'Conner has his reasons. I don't know them. But Mrs. O'Conner was very upset about the coffee spill. Once she changed, she seemed fine. She left for a lunch with a friend of

Pick Your Potion

hers about noon. Nothing was wrong with her," she said.

"That's good. So, nothing happened here to upset her. Nothing weird. No arguments. No enemies?" I asked.

"Of course not. She's worked her part-time for years. We have a nice calm group of people who love books. That's all," Mrs. Drew said.

"Do you know who she had lunch with?" I asked.

Mrs. Drew shook her head. "A friend. They went to the Italian place on the corner. She came back and worked until about two. That was it. She never complained of anything. Being tired or her food disagreeing with her. I've seen her get a bit ill in the past if she misses a meal or needs a bit more insulin, but she was on top of it and had all her stuff with her always."

"So, she'd been ill before. What happened? I mean, what if she couldn't take care of herself?" I asked.

"Audrey also has diabetes, so she knew how to take blood sugar. And depending on the results, it was either she'd need juice or insulin. But Mrs. O'Conner was so on top of her condition it was never necessary. She only told us because of her grandson. He has Type 1, as well. She made us all take a first aid class and gave us her own class on diabetes. We do a summer program with a lot of kids and some after school programs, as well, so she wanted to know her grandson was safe, even if she wasn't working that day." Mrs. Drew sighed sharply.

104

"I understand her caring about her grandson. Kids don't want to take care of themselves. But I'm sure she taught him to be responsible," I said.

Mrs. Drew tilted her head in a way that said she didn't fully agree. "He isn't so young. Eighth grade, I believe. He resents being sick. Avoided talking to her when he would come for programs. But what kid wants their grandma fussing over them when they're with their friends?"

"I understand. But you ladies aren't nurses. It's good to know what you can do, but it's dangerous to mess with someone else's medication. I don't think I could do that unless it was family," I admitted.

"I agree. Luckily, we haven't had that issue come up. The point is there was no sign of her being ill at all that day. She was cold and couldn't get warm, but a lot of people were saying that. It was bitter cold, and the wind whipped through people," she said.

"It is a serious winter. If that's all you remember, I'll get out of your hair," I said.

She sipped her coffee. "That's all. But thanks for the morning java," she said.

"Sure." I grabbed my purse and headed out of her office.

Audrey was sitting behind the desk. For some reason, I paused and wanted to chat with her a bit. She didn't make eye contact, so my instinct said there was something to talk about.

"Hi, Audrey. Mind if I ask you a couple things?" I asked.

She looked around and shrugged. "Mrs. Drew probably covered it all."

Pick Your Potion

"I know. The big stuff. She mentioned you were also a diabetic and knew how to test blood and all of that. So, you might notice even better if Mrs. O'Conner had any signs that she wasn't feeling great when she was at work that day. Or if I missed something," I said.

Audrey shook her head. "She was fine. She generally wanted to be left alone and even more on that day."

"Just a bad day?" I asked.

She lifted a shoulder. "She and I didn't really get along, so she didn't confide in me."

"Mrs. Drew made it sound like you were her diabetic backup," I replied.

"That was her way of forgetting about it. Mrs. O'Conner always picked on me for my eating habits. She was rail thin, and I'm not." Audrey blushed.

She was a bit plump, but I could see Mrs. O'Conner being a bit critical. "She picked on you?"

"If I ate better, exercised more—I could get rid of my diabetes. She never could. I don't know why it was such a big deal to her. I've always had bad asthma, and it made even gym glass hard." She sniffled.

"Don't feel bad. I know she said some harsh things to me and my baristas, at times. But all that proves is she was unhappy and took it out on others. Did she have any real enemies here?" I asked.

"Well, she picked on me. Everyone else just avoided her. Mrs. Drew would be the closest thing to an enemy, but that was just Mrs. O'Conner

106

resenting that they didn't give her the top job," Audrey said.

"But she only works part-time," I said.

Audrey nodded. "She wanted the top job and full-time work. Her husband was retired, and he was older. He was on Medicare, but she wasn't sixty-five yet when the job was decided. I think she is, now. Anyway, she wanted it for the benefits. But when they talked to the staff, no one wanted to work for her. Mrs. Drew is strict and dull but fair and not critical."

"Much better. So, Mrs. Drew would have no reason to hurt her," I said.

"Hurt her? We all thought it was natural causes," Audrey said. Her eyebrows shot up in worry.

"Well, the police are looking around for clues or enemies. Maybe they know something they won't tell us," I fibbed.

"You think?" she asked.

I shrugged. "I've talked to all my staff, and no one did anything to her drink. I mean, if someone had added a bunch of sugar she hadn't ordered, she'd have tasted it. If they'd used real sugar instead of an artificial sweetener, she'd feel it. But, obviously, that wasn't the case because she didn't get ill when she was here. It'd affect her fairly quickly, right? If someone did that?"

She nodded. "In a drink, definitely. But she always has her testing kit and insulin with her, so she'd just dose. She had her garden club later and dinner with her family. It sounds like she made it through all those things, so odds are it was natural causes in the night."

Pick Your Potion

"Probably. Thanks. I just wanted to be sure she didn't get sick after she left my place. I didn't want to ignore a problem if there was one," I explained.

"You sound like a great boss. But I think you're good. I should get back to work." Audrey looked around.

"Of course, sorry. Blame me for asking a million questions. One more. Do you know who she was having lunch with that day?" I couldn't help but try.

"A friend. Olive?" She frowned. "I think."

"Thanks." I waved as I left.

Chapter Twelve

Walking to the front door of my café, I barely looked at Mr. O'Conner, who didn't bother trying to protest my going in.

"Please go home or I will call the police. You're shivering," I said as I pulled the door behind me against the nasty winter wind.

He didn't move.

I walked into the busy café and met three people waiting for my attention with issues that had nothing to do with coffee or tea.

Aunt Mandy came up first. "Ryan is over the infection. He wants to help. To work or something. Vinny told him he can't leave, now. Not with the police around."

I nodded. "He can do inventory if he wants, but he's not allowed up here."

"If we could pass him off as a new hire, we might could move him on quicker," she said.

"They'll see him leave but never arrive. You think they won't notice that? No. Sorry, he stays down there or I'll lock him up," I said.

Esme walked up next. "Nothing?"

"Nothing really. But Mrs. O'Conner was fine at the library and through lunch, so there's no indication whatever it is came from us with any delay. She wasn't sick. No one saw her dose with insulin or anything."

"Good. The coven is grumbling about this." Esme headed to my table, and I followed her.

Pick Your Potion

Margaret came over with my usual hot coffee. "Thanks," I said.

Once Margaret was gone, I asked Esme, "What are they complaining about? I'm trying to make sure we're in the clear."

We sat, and I took a long drink of warming mocha-flavored coffee.

Esme sighed. "They think Mr. O'Conner is making such a fuss that he's the one behind the threats. He staged them."

"Staged them?" I asked, trying to wrap my brain around that motive.

"Before his wife died. Once he knew she was so upset, maybe he thought it'd be good to get us in trouble. So, he had someone leave the messages and write the note. He planned to have it rattle his wife and she'd go to the police. Get us in trouble, and his wife would have something to keep her busy and feel like she was justified."

"That's awful. Making up a threat. I don't see him doing that just for fun."

Esme gave me a look that said I was naive. "If Mrs. O'Conner is this much trouble for a coffee shop she's in a few minutes a day, imagine what a headache she is to her husband."

I opened my mouth, but instead of words, I drank some coffee and mulled over the idea. She didn't seem to be sweet to anyone.

"But he's so devoted to her. Why protest us now if he knows we didn't do anything?"

"He doesn't want them to find out it was an inside fake threat. Once the medical stuff comes back, he'll probably stop, and the case will close." Esme shrugged. "It's a theory."

"Well, Mrs. O'Conner's boss didn't like her much. Mrs. O'Conner wanted the boss' job and didn't get it. But the boss seems like she was stuck with the grouchy part-timer. I could twist that into a motive if I wanted to." I swirled my coffee cup to mix up the flavor.

"We could say your need to investigate is a way of throwing suspicion off of you." Esme shook her head.

"If they didn't know me, maybe. I'm trying to help people. I used all the money my parents left me to open this café so we had a place for the coven to meet and a way to tap into human conversations. I want to keep the peace and help everyone." I took another swig of my coffee.

"Well, the coven wants to believe you put the paranormal beings first. You have a soft spot for humans."

"We're witches. We're humans with powers. My aunt and uncle have no powers. My cousins think they might have some, but none have shown up, and they're eighteen," I said softly.

"We all know that. You and your mother were the powerful line. You really should be thinking about finding a powerful wizard and continuing that line," Esme said with a grin.

I frowned and slowly set my cup down to avoid dropping it. "You want to talk about me having kids? Why don't you have some first?"

"I can't. I can't spend half of my time as a cat and be pregnant. The baby wouldn't shift so I'd be stuck as a human and lose my nine lives."

"Or have a litter of kittens. Would they have your shifting power?" I asked.

Pick Your Potion

"No, and I'm not having kittens," she whispered through her teeth.

We were at the back table near the kitchen. All the good tables were on the other side, and the nearest one was five feet away. The only ones who might overhear anything were staff, and the loudness of the machines and the TV piping in a witch movie made sure they couldn't overhear us.

"That sucks. Do you want kids?" I asked.

She shook her head. "My dad took off on my mom. I like men, but children are a burden," Esme said.

I bit my lip. I'd always felt like a burden to my aunt and uncle, and I wasn't even their kid. They hadn't chosen to have me the way they'd tried to have the twins. My aunt hadn't been able to become pregnant again after Violent and Iris.

"You okay?" Esme asked.

"Yeah. My aunt and uncle never made me feel like burden, even though I certainly was."

"No, that's different. That's stepping up and taking care of your family. If something happened to them, I would've taken care of you and the twins. I'm only a distant cousin of your mother and aunt, but that's what family does." She patted my hand.

"I'm only twenty-five—I'm not in a rush to have a bunch of magical kids to deal with. I mean, there isn't a Hogwarts to ship them off to." That would really be nice.

She laughed. "True. You were always moving things with your mind, just because you could."

"What brought on this baby talk?" I asked.

Esme shrugged. "I think of the future of the coven. Of the paranormal people. We need powerful people to step up like you have. And consolidating power would only help you."

"So, the paranormal world is as sexist as the rest of humanity?" I asked.

Esme glared at me. "No and yes. Wicca and many pagan religions elevate women and the Goddess. Mother Earth. But, face it, power wins. A vampire king. A pack of strong male werewolves. Those aren't things to be discounted. If you had a husband who was as strong as you, there would be less grumbling and questioning. You'd have a united front."

"I don't mind being questioned. I'm not all-knowing. I can take the input and doubt and learn from it. But if I run into any super-hot wizards worth procreating with, I'll let you know," I said.

"I have a couple in mind," Esme said.

"Then, you have some fun with them," I said.

"I have my share of fun. I'm thinking of the future, long term, and so should you," she said.

"I'm not going to live as long as you will. I'm just thinking about Mrs. O'Conner and that hunter in my basement." The twins walked in. "Oh, I need to talk to the twins. Nag me later, okay?"

Esme sighed and walked to the basement stairs. I caught her shifting out of the corner of my eye. She'd pout for a bit and get over it. I was too young to get married. There was no way I'd get married just to produce ultra-powerful little witches. Kids were a lot of work, and I wasn't in a rush.

Pick Your Potion

The twins sat and removed their gloves and scarves. "Hi," they said in unison.

"Hey, sorry to drag you back here. How's classes?" I asked.

"Fine," they said, again together.

"We're done for today," Iris said.

"Cool. I just wanted to ask out about who Mrs. O'Conner might've had lunch with the day of her death. All I could get was where and the name Olive," I said.

"I got this. Get me some tea?" Violet asked her twin.

Iris headed for the counter.

"Everything okay?" I asked.

Violet nodded. "Dating as a twin is tricky. Guys don't get it. And when they can't tell us apart, it's really weird."

"Yikes, another reason I'm glad I wasn't a twin," I said.

"You a twin? That'd be awesome. Double the powers." She smiled and pulled out her tablet. "I remember someone named Olive on her friend list in Facebook. Old people."

"Facebook is old, now?" I didn't really do social media. The café had a page that we made sure was updated, quirky, and fun, but I didn't feel the need to share.

She laughed. "When grandparents are doing it, yes. Get Snapchat."

"Isn't that for sexting?" I asked.

"It's grown beyond that," she replied.

"I'm good. Do you have info on Olive?" I asked.

114

"Olive Reynolds. Widowed. Lives not far from here. Why do people put so much info out there?" She sighed.

I pulled out my phone and Googled the name. Her address popped up. "Got her. Thanks! I'd have spent all afternoon on Mrs. O'Conner's Facebook to find that. And you guys did all the work already."

Iris returned with two big cups of tea. "Good?"

"I got what I need. Thanks. You two stay warm. Do your homework," I said.

"You're such a mom. Be more of a sister," Iris said.

I shuddered at being called a mom. "Fine. Hit a party and drink until you puke. But don't blame me when your dad tracks you down and raises hell. He never let me have too much fun as a teenager."

"You didn't go to college," Violet said.

"Vi," Iris said.

"It's okay. I didn't. Esme thought it was more important for me to work on powers, and I did. But I also worked part-time in coffee shops. So, I was sort of training on how to run this. Not everyone is college material, but you two are super smart, so don't blow it. There is plenty of time for guys when you've got a degree," I said.

"Such a mom," they said in unison.

"Thanks, I needed that." I pulled my gloves out of my pocket and suited up for the blustery outside. "I need to go bug Olive Reynolds."

Pick Your Potion

Part of me wanted to use a truth potion on these women, but if I did, they'd remember all of the questions. If I used a memory spell on them, it might work. But they might get suspicious if they couldn't remember what we talked about. Magic worked for some, but for now, I had to try it the human way. The house was pleasant-looking on the outside. It had a cottage feel, and the street was quiet. A murderer couldn't live here. At least, that's how it felt.

I knocked on the door, and a stern woman opened it.

"Can I help you?" she asked.

"I'm sorry to just show up. My name is Claudia Crestwood. I own the Witch's Brew coffee shop. Mrs. O'Conner was a regular customer. And I understand that she was a friend of yours," I said.

I extended my hand, but she just looked at it.

"What about her?" she asked.

"As you might know, her husband is blaming my café for her death. I was hoping to find a friend of his to talk some sense into him. He's standing out in front of my café, freezing. He's risking his health for nothing," I said.

"You know it's nothing?" she asked.

I nodded. "I checked with the library. Mrs. O'Conner was fine there. If we'd done anything, she's have been sick."

"Really. There are slow-acting poisons, I'm sure." She eyed me coldly.

"We'll have to wait for the tox screen for that proof, but I don't know anything about poison," I said.

CC Dragon

"Just potions. Why don't you come in? For some tea. Warm up," she said.

"Thanks." I felt like I was walking into something I wasn't ready for, but at least it was warm.

I stomped the snow off my boots. I was pointed to a proper living room for entertaining with no TV and uncomfortable furniture. I chose an armchair on one side of a cute little wooden table.

I cast a warming spell on my hands and feet while waiting for Mrs. Reynolds to bring out the tea. I hadn't expected to be on the porch for so long.

Mrs. Reynolds brought out a tray with a fussy ceramic tea set that looked older than I was. She was being polite when I felt like she didn't want me there. She poured the tea and handed me a cup.

"Thank you. So, you don't like our potions?" I asked.

"My niece is a Wiccan. Pagan. Or whatever. She lives in New York City. Don't think I'm prejudiced. Martha O'Conner criticized everyone and everything. Her husband, her daughter, and her grandson." She sipped her tea with pursed lips.

"And her friends?" I asked.

She nodded. "Her friends, too. But she never was nasty enough to make anyone want to kill. She took care of herself. I suspect her husband is just so shocked. No one thought she could ever die. The woman would have a setback and

Pick Your Potion

recover. She'd come back stronger. We never thought she'd die before any of us. It's a shame."

"So, you don't know anyone who really wanted to hurt her?" I asked.

"No. Her husband is upset and lost, honestly. She wore the pants in that family. I've invited him over for dinner, if that helps. I can try to help him forge a new routine. See his grandson, his daughter, and so on. He'll need a cleaning lady. I can help him find one. And take him to the grocery store. Help him with those habits." She sipped her tea.

"That's very nice of you. Maybe you can help him see we didn't do anything to hurt her. She had a bad day, but we're not out to hurt our customers." I enjoyed the hot drink.

"He told me about the threats. That someone left messages. I'm sure it wasn't you. You're a businesswoman. I understand that. I respect that. I worked in the office at my late husband's dental practice. I know what it's like when patients aren't happy. Customers are the same. But someone in your little witch group got out of hand. You need to take control. Be the boss if that's what you are."

"I'm not the boss of all the witches in Hartford. If someone was offended by her comments, that doesn't mean I'm responsible for their actions. Mr. O'Conner wants a scapegoat. I'm not going to be it. The police will get the results soon, but my business could be ruined before then. We're seeing fewer customers. If you can convince Mr. O'Conner to stop protesting, that'd be wonderful," I said.

118

"I'm not sure I have that sort of influence," she lied with a sweet smile.

A shiver ran down my back. She was moving in on the widower a bit fast.

"I think if you compare it to your late husband's business, I think he might. Some people must've lost a tooth or had a bad time. Things can't always go perfectly. If those patients had protested outside of the office, that seriously could've ruined his reputation. Is it fair to do that to others without real proof?" I asked.

She shook her head and stiffened her spine. "Your shop has a good reputation. Martha hated seeing chains all over the city. She'd be upset if your place went under because of her husband's grief. I'll try."

"Thank you." Things had taken a turn, but if she could help and was willing to, I could use it.

Did she have a motive? She seemed to have a big interest in Mr. O'Conner, but was that motive for murder?

"How long were you friends with Mrs. O'Conner?" I asked.

"Oh, forever. High school. She and I competed over everything."

"Did you always win?"

"It was usually a tie. I got head cheerleader, and she got homecoming queen. That sort of thing. We both married men with good careers. I was a little more set than she was, but my husband died. I didn't want to win this way." She poured more tea.

I checked out her jewelry. It looked like she'd won. But she didn't seem the type of woman to kill

Pick Your Potion

for it. She probably wanted to win with a clear conscience. I'd gone to school with girls like that. "I never had a chance of winning in high school. The popular girls made fun of my hair and my aunt's hippie ways. They asked what happened to my parents. They were normal, and that made them win. I never wanted to be a cheerleader. Homecoming queen? Maybe for a few seconds, but you can't expect votes when you don't participate."

"No Wiccan club?" she asked.

I shrugged. "I was already in a real coven. I had two educations going on. But I'm happy, so that stuff didn't matter in the end."

"No? What happened to your parents?" she asked.

"They died when I was young. But I had my aunt and uncle, plus two cousins. My mom and aunt were both sort of the odd ones in the family," I admitted.

"And you lost her. No wonder you didn't want to join in in high school. Probably no close friends?" she asked.

"Not really. No. I had friends but not close." I downed another cup of tea, this time without taking my time.

"I'm not surprised. You lost your parents. You were afraid to get attached to new people. Afraid they'd leave you just like your parents did," she said.

"I had my family." It couldn't be that simple.

"Yes, you still had family taking care of you, and you loved them. It'd be hard to lose them. So, why add people to the list of ones who could hurt you? I don't blame you. And, now, you're worried your business could be taken from you."

"Was your husband a dentist or a shrink?" I asked.

She smiled. "You'd be surprised how much people share at a dentist's office. I held a lot of hands. Heard a lot of crazy reasons why people feared the dentist. The pain. The genetic problems. Emergencies. You see people when they are very vulnerable. No one likes the dentist unless they have naturally strong and pretty teeth. Don't worry; I'll talk to Mr. O'Conner. Hopefully, the police will close the case soon, but I can try to talk some sense into that man."

"Thanks. I should get back to the coffee shop," I said.

"Bundle up; it's cold." She walked me to the door.

Did I keep people at a distance to keep from being hurt? I never dated guys seriously. I dated, but I was never interested in relationships. I hiked out to my car and cranked up the heat as I headed back to the café. I had to deal with this work problem and then Ryan. When I got free time, I'd worry about friends and boyfriends.

Pick Your Potion

Chapter Thirteen

I was dead to the world when a vampire came pounding on my bedroom door. Snuggling under the blankets, I never wanted to move. After a day out in the harsh weather, I was finally warm, again.

"What?" I shouted.

"It's Brad. You need to get out here. Your guest is trying to leave," he said.

"Damn. Stop him. I'll be right there." I swung my legs out and shoved my feet right into the fuzzy boots. My flannel pajama pants, a gift from the twins, had frogs with little crowns on them. Some were making kissy faces, and some were winking. My cousins and I didn't have the same taste, but the pants were warm. My legs always got cold first, but a long tank top worked just fine because my shoulders never seemed to get chilly.

I ran my fingers through my hair then grabbed a big black sweater, just in case the fight had moved outside.

I hustled down the stairs and found two other vamps blocking Ryan's exit. He was at the top of the basement stairs. Perfect. Right where customers could see and hear him.

"Tell these walking dead things with dental issues to get out of my way," Ryan yelled.

"You're not leaving. Not with the police around."

Pick Your Potion

"I can't stay down there another minute. I'm going crazy," he said.

"Then, you should've left before this mess happened. I can't help it. Get back down there and go to sleep." I folded my arms.

"Hey, I tried to escape but you wouldn't let me. I could help clean up here. I could learn to make coffee," he offered.

"You just insulted my staff. You hunt vampires—they don't want to work with you. I don't trust you to work with them." I waved my hand at him; that shoved him back a few steps.

"Big tough witch. That's all you've got?" he mocked.

I went to the landline, while the vamps continued to cover Ryan, and called my uncle.

"He's getting stir crazy," he said.

"I know. I'm about to lock him up. He won't cooperate." I didn't want to upset my uncle, but he had to take some responsibility for what he'd taken in and dumped on me.

"I'll be there in the morning and keep him busy during the day. You can't let him do something at night?" my uncle asked.

"I can't be up all night babysitting him and the vampires. That mix will not go well," I pointed out.

"Right. Fine. Do what you need to do to keep him under control. Night." He hung up.

"Great." I hung up the phone as the bell jingled over the door.

The wind gusted in, and I wrapped my sweater around me.

I nodded to the vamps to go deal with the customer. When I looked over to see who it was, I expected a college student on deadline or utility workers out repairing lines. We got a lot of cops and firemen who needed refueling overnight. Sometimes, nurses and EMTs. This man was none of those. He was in a dark suit with his hair slicked back. His watch was expensive, but there was something more. He was powerful. Not human power. My kind of power. I knew him.

He ordered a dark roast black with a double shot of no sleep potion.

"You'll be up all night," I warned him.

"I do my best work at night." He didn't smile. "You're Claudia Crestwood?"

"I am. Have we met?" I asked.

"I believe so, but it's been a long time. Your cousin mentioned you were having some human problems. I might be able to help," he offered.

"I've got two human problems, right now, but no, thanks. I can handle it. What cousin?" I asked.

"Esmeralda. She and my aunt are very good friends. Very old friends," he said.

"So, your aunt does the nine lives thing, too?" I asked.

He nodded. "That is a small group. I hear you're almost as powerful as your cousin. Or me."

I showed no reaction. "I'm strong enough. I'm just trying to handle my human problems without major magic. I don't want to untangle a mess by causing a bigger one."

Ryan watched from the doorway on the top step. I should lock him up. I cast a spell to cover

Pick Your Potion

my butt, any non-magical people would forget anything they saw in the shop, including Ryan.

"You're right. Some witches use magic too publicly or frequently and get caught up in trying to cover their tracks. Exposure is dangerous," the customer agreed.

"Exactly. I have a customer who died, and our spell says it was not natural causes. But the police think it was. They're looking into it. I'm trying to find the killer, so the widower will stop protesting my shop. And so I can get rid of my other human problem," I glanced back at the doorway.

"He is staring a lot. A former lover you don't like?" he asked.

I laughed. "Hardly. A hunter who got caught by humans, and my uncle is giving him sanctuary in my shop."

"Ryan Jones." The hunter stepped out from the shadows and extended a hand, introducing himself to the customer. The vampires behind the counter moved to drag Ryan down the stairs, but I shook my head at them. We didn't need a big incident in front of customers.

I tried to place the wizard. Remember his name. He hadn't been at school with me. From what he claimed about his aunt and Esme, he was one of the Killean family that could trace their line back to the Druids. They were handsome, powerful, and not very social. So far, this man hit all the marks. He was a year or two older than me, I'd guess.

"Bran Killean," he replied without shaking hands.

126

"Bran? Like *Game of Thrones*? You poor thing," I stifled a giggle.

"The Celtic name means king or raven, so it's a pretty obvious name choice for Mr. Martin since the boy chases a raven around. My middle name is no better, so Bran is it." He took his coffee and sipped it.

"I haven't seen you in here," I said.

"You sleep at night," Brad said, grinning at Bran like a fool. He'd been a step or two behind the hunter, watching him like a hawk.

I rolled my eyes. "You're a vampire, Mr. Killean?"

"No. I deal with people all day and get my work done best at night. I catnap. But I don't want to interrupt your late-night tryst." He grinned slightly.

I looked down and laughed. "Yeah. My best lingerie. Please. This hunter keeps trying to escape."

"So, let him go. Or is he a frog you turned into a prince, but he's not up to snuff?" Bran asked.

"My cousins gave me these pajamas. They're warm. This hunter has to stay. The police are probably still watching the building. It's a long story, but we saved him, and he's got to deal with helping us," I said.

"You wanted me gone as soon as I was healthy enough. I'm healthy," he said. "Help me get out of here, and I'll do anything you want."

Bran's eyebrow raised at that offer. For a split-second, I thought he might be gay. That'd be my luck. Any guy who captured my interest was gay, taken, or a bad boy, as my aunt called them.

Pick Your Potion

"What could you possibly do for me?" Bran asked.

"The Killeans are a powerful magical family, Ryan. They don't need you any more than I do," I said.

"Maybe he's strong enough to make me invisible. The police never saw me enter, but they don't have to see me leave either. And make it last for a while so I can get far away." Ryan nodded.

"I'm sure Ms. Crestwood is strong enough to render you invisible. She has her reasons for keeping you around. Maybe you'd run to the police or get her in trouble, somehow." Bran shook his head at Ryan.

Then, Bran snapped his fingers. Ryan passed out right there on the floor.

"Why did you do that?" I asked.

"I was bored with him. He's a user. He thinks he's noble, but the only hunters I trust are gypsies, like your uncle. These types are in it for the kill." Bran looked down his nose at Ryan.

"I felt the same way, but my uncle brought him here. I couldn't say no. And then, the customer thing happened. I don't need him being caught by the police or followed back here if he needs something. He'll make it worse, even if I made him permanently invisible," I said.

"Then, you should keep him locked up. A human with a superiority complex is more dangerous than an untamed vampire." Bran stared at my legs, again.

"Sorry, I wasn't expecting company." I tugged my sweater lower to try and cover the goofy pajama pants. "My cousins and I have very different styles. But I can't hurt their feelings."

"Those are not from Esmeralda." He laughed.

His booming laugh sent a rush through me. "No, not Esme. My uncle's children. I was raised by my aunt and uncle. They have a set of twins, only eighteen, now. I got these a couple Christmases ago. Appropriate for a single girl or a single witch."

"Still searching for Prince Charming? There has to be a better story than that." He stepped over Ryan's limp body. "Tell me."

"I'm the boss here, Mr. Killean, not you. Brad will get you another drink of your choice on the house for the trouble. I'll get Ryan down to a cell," I said.

"I don't need a free coffee. I need to know about the frogs," he said.

I almost turned around and snapped at him. But there was a longing, a sadness about him that made me pause. "You tell anyone, and I'll deny and make you pay."

He didn't look scared. But if he knew Esme, he knew how powerful I was. My guess was he was one of her choices for me.

"Promise," I said.

"Who would I tell?" he asked.

"Senior prom. My date was just a guy who asked me. I wasn't dating him. I didn't know him well, but it meant so much to my aunt that I go. Have the prom experience and all the pictures. It made her happy. He was all hands and lips. Like I was supposed to sleep with him because it was prom. I turned him into a frog on the ride home

Pick Your Potion

and sent the limo back to his parents' house like that." I shrugged.

"He stayed that way for how long?" Bran asked.

"A couple hours at least. His parents were freaking out. They thought he'd been kidnapped. They put the frog in the yard. I swore up and down he was fine when he dropped me off. A perfect gentleman, which was a lie. But I wasn't going to any after parties with him. I hinted he may have gone drinking with a few friends after he dropped me off. Finally, he turned human in the backyard. Naked. He was confused. His parents thought he'd gotten plastered and went wild with his friends. They grounded him for a week." I couldn't hide my smile.

"Transfiguration at that level. Of a human. For that long, impressive for a seventeen year old," he said.

"My aunt was mad at me. Exposure. Do no harm. Sometimes, I can't help myself, but I try not to use my powers without thinking it through." I looked down at Ryan. "I don't trust him enough to let him loose, yet."

"Trust those instincts. We're at war with humanity in some ways. We can never forget that," he said.

I shook my head. "My aunt and cousins have no powers. Esme does, of course, but my uncle is a human gypsy. I don't want to fight humans."

"I don't either. But if they knew the full extent of our world, we would be at war. We're more powerful than they are."

"Yet we don't seek to dominate them," I said.

"Evolution has its advantages. But I do appreciate your work here. Your involvement with humans keeps us all informed. It's a great service, and if I can be of help to you, just call." He handed me a card.

"I don't inform you of anything." I took the card anyway.

"Esmeralda does. What's necessary. There is a network of information. We appreciate it." He looked around. "It's a lovely shop."

"What do you do?" I asked.

"My family owns several businesses," he said stealthily.

"That makes you a Soprano? Is there a paranormal mob? I never heard of that," I said.

He laughed. "No? Well, I suppose, if there was one, we'd be it. If you cross my family, you'll pay. Much like, if someone crossed you, he'd be a frog."

I felt my cheeks burn. "I can do a lot worse, now."

"I'm sure of it. We own a funeral home. A car dealership. A lawn and snow service company. A yarn and craft store my aunt insisted on that is actually turning a profit."

"That's convenient. Pick what you want to do, and the family buys you a business." I knew they had money, but that's big, big money.

"Not quite. You have to pay your dues working in a family business and make a proposal for a new one. We make our money honestly; we always have. Invest it wisely. We don't bother others, and they don't bother us. We do deal with humans as customers, so I understand, but we

Pick Your Potion

tend to use magic to resolve things quicker. Your approach is unique."

"It sounds so calm." I envied him.

"Your life sounds like an adventure. I hope your human death case is resolved." He finished his coffee and tossed the cup in the trash.

"Thanks. I'm trying to solve it myself, but doing things the human way sucks." I rubbed my neck. "I need to get this one locked up and get back to bed. I need more than a catnap."

"Of course. But if you had something from all the suspects, you could scry for the killer," he suggested.

"I could. But getting an item isn't easy. And with more than one person in a location as a suspect, it would only help so much." I shrugged.

"Do you need any help?" He pointed Ryan.

I chuckled and waved my hand. His limp body swiftly lifted off the ground. I guided him down the stairs and into a cell. I didn't look back to see if Bran was impressed or not. He wasn't what I expected from the Killean family. I'd heard they were snobs who looked down on families like mine, those with non-magical members. Also families that socialized with humans too much and willingly weren't big with the paranormal royalty. My line was old and strong, but I couldn't trace it back to Stonehenge. That stuff didn't matter to me. The idea of Bran mowing a lawn or selling cars on his summer breaks from school made me smile. Maybe Esme had better taste in men than I'd given her credit for.

Chapter Fourteen

That morning, I had the same drink Bran had plus vanilla creamer. The caffeine jolt helped. It'd been hard to get back to sleep after such a weird first encounter. The PJs hadn't helped, but I wasn't a Goth girl. I didn't sport a witch style all the time. Okay, the frogs were lame. But it was a gift and warm.

Today, I was in all black: big black boots that went to my knees, leggings that kept me warm and a black with gray trim sweater dress that came to the edge of the boots and down to my elbows.

"Why is Ryan locked up?" my aunt asked softly as she sat at my table.

"He tried to escape last night. Attacked some vamps. I don't need him lashing out. I called Uncle Vinny. He's supposed to come over today and help soothe the savage hunter." I rolled my eyes.

"He wants you to make him invisible," she said.

"He said that last night, too. No, I can't trust him. I wish Vin wouldn't associate with non-gypsy hunters. They go rogue too much." I shook my head.

"Fine. I hope this case is over soon." She went off in a foul mood.

I wasn't in a better one. I had to meet the garden club today. I'd checked that the meeting

Pick Your Potion

was still scheduled, given that gardening wasn't really popular in the winter. But they still met, so I was going. They had a room at the local social center, so it wasn't like pushing in on Mrs. Reynolds in her home.

I watched the front. No Mr. O'Conner yet today, but it was early.

Esme sat across from me with a smug expression.

"What? Did you kill Ryan? I won't tell. Give the body to the cops," I said.

She pointed at me. "That's the sort of dark humor that makes people worry about you. You're normal some of the time and then sound positively evil."

"It's a quirky sense of humor. That's all." I shrugged and checked my messages on my phone.

"I heard that Bran Killean came by last night," she said.

I nodded. "I guess he comes by a lot at night when I'm asleep. Ryan tried to run, so I had to deal with that."

"Sounds like you made an impression," Esme smiled.

"Froggy PJ bottoms and a bulky black sweater with winter boots. I'm sure I did." I put his card information into my phone. "Who does cards, anymore?"

"Polite people. You don't have to wait for someone to put in the info and repeat it ten times. You hand over the card, and they can input the info or not. You're smart to keep him on file." She grabbed the card. "He's good looking."

134

CC Dragon

"If you've got your eye on him, don't worry about me. Strictly paranormal connections." I smiled.

"Really, Claudia. You bumped into one of the men I'd love to see you with. I knew he came here, but you don't think I could've maneuvered Ryan to misbehave just when Bran was about to come in," she said.

I sat back. "I didn't say when Ryan acted up."

"Of course you did. Or Brad did. Someone must've told me." She waved it off.

"You did something. You put a spell on Ryan to act up when Bran came within so far of the shop?" I couldn't believe it, but it made more sense than Ryan suddenly trying to run when he knew the vampires would stop him. He didn't have a weapon to take out the vamps. If he was serious about leaving, he'd have made a stake out of the old wooden crates we had in the basement.

Esme sighed. "Okay, fine, I did help a little. But Bran comes in so often. His aunt says how much he loves your place. The coffee, the service, and the feel of the place. I wanted you two to meet. And it's cute you weren't your perfectly pulled together self. You intimidate men."

"If I do, then those men are weak. And I'm not always perfectly pulled together. Most of the time here, I wear jeans and a T-shirt for the shop with coffee stains on it."

"Your hair is always perfect," she said.

My black hair was thick and pin straight. "If I wanted it to curl, it wouldn't be perfect."

"That's why you and Bran would be great for each other. You accept yourselves and try to help

Pick Your Potion

people. You're not out trying to be something you're not. Or pretending the world will hand you everything. Your generation has a lot of challenges, but you two weren't coddled the way most kids your age were."

I stared at her. "You think the twins were coddled?"

She nodded. "Your aunt never tried to change you. She guided you, raised you, but you were so like your mother and she missed her so letting you be you was more important. And you'd witnessed your mother's death. You had scars she couldn't erase. Trauma the twins couldn't imagine, even now. It makes you stronger as a person. The magic, that's impressive, too," Esme said.

"Hardly impressive to you. But I keep trying," I said.

"You impressed Bran. And he told his aunt already. She texted me. You need someone to push you and challenge you—that's me. But your man should always admire you." Esme checked her phone.

"You and his aunt. This is a full-on setup. He's okay with that?" I asked.

"He's a man. He thinks it's all his idea. He ran into you, and you're so this and that. He might have magic, but he's still a lovable goofy man who thinks he's the cleverest guy in the room." She grinned.

"Then, I'll tell him what his aunt is up to, and it'll be done." I picked up my phone.

Esme waved her hand and knocked my phone across the room.

"You break it, you buy me a new one," I said.

A customer brought it over before I could go searching.

"Thanks; I'm a klutz today," I said.

"It's fine," she said.

My phone rang, and Esme perked up.

I answered. "Hello, Detective Shelley," I said.

Esme's grin disappeared.

"Ms. Crestwood. I wanted to let you know that there was nothing found in the tox screen. No illegal drugs. No poison. Nothing, really. Her usual pain meds for arthritis and her sleeping pill, but nothing out of the ordinary. I've let Mr. O'Conner know, so hopefully, he will relax a bit on protesting your shop," she said.

"Thanks. That makes me feel better. Nothing for the autopsy?" I asked.

"A couple more days. The ME was on vacation for the holidays, and so, we had a backup who was very green and slow. Then, all this cold weather, you get people dying while shoveling a drive. Or lifting salt bags into their truck. The results will be good; we just need to be a bit more patient," she said.

"Thanks. Please let me know if there is anything I can do. Bye." I ended the call.

"No poison. She wasn't shot or stabbed. No one said anything about bruising."

"Smothered," Esme said.

"That means someone had to get into her house," I said.

"Well, you keep doing what you're doing. Your aunt and I will deal with Ryan. But don't be too hard on him," she said.

Pick Your Potion

"I won't, now that I know it's you. For the record, Bran knocked him out—magically. I levitated him down there. If he's complaining," I said.

"You and Bran sound like a good team," she said.

"I'm leaving," I said. I went over to Ellen, head barista on the shift. "Call if you need anything. If Mr. O'Conner shows up, call the cops. It's not even going to hit zero today."

"Gotcha, boss," Ellen said.

"Don't pick that up from the guys. They're just weird." I smiled. The vamps called me boss, and Ellen must be hanging around with them. She was a witch with enough powers that I didn't worry about her as much.

"They're different and cute," she replied.

What was it about vampires? I saw nothing cute or hot about vamps or weres. Those were things that had been done to them. Someone turned them into a vampire or a werewolf. Okay, you could be born a werewolf, but that was rare. Witches and wizards had to work at their powers and grow them. I'd rather earn my powers than be a victim. I felt sorry for vamps and werewolves...but right now, I needed to help Mrs. O'Conner and find out who'd hurt her.

I strolled into the social center a few blocks away. There were several meeting rooms and a board listing all the groups and when they met. I felt very antisocial when I saw all of the groups. Book clubs, sewing clubs, and even a beginning Wiccan class that I had no knowledge of. I took a

138

picture of that post with my phone, so I could follow up later on.

Putting that out of my head, I found the room for the garden club and slipped in. There were five women in the room, and they looked at me carefully.

"Can we help you?" asked one of them.

"Hi, I'm Claudia. I own the Witch's Brew café. I understand Mrs. O'Conner was a member here?"

A few of the women exchanged looks, but one patted the seat next to her. "I'm Sara. Martha was a member. She had the most beautiful roses and exotic items. Do you garden?" she asked.

"No, I don't really. I just came by, because I was so sorry to hear about Mrs. O'Conner, and I wondered if anyone heard anything, yet. I know her husband is very upset." I played dumb. With this many women, one was bound to want to be a know-it-all.

"He blames you," another woman said.

"Claudia, this is Kate. That's Joyce, Misty, and Fran." Sara made the introductions around the table. All the women were in their fifties or sixties, except for Misty.

"I know he blames the café, Kate. But that's why I've been checking up on her friends and other things she did that day. She was fine at her job at the library and at lunch with her friends. So, whatever made her ill, I don't think it came from my shop. I really hope the police and medical tests give us the answers as soon as possible. She was a regular customer, and I'd hate for people to

Pick Your Potion

believe we're dangerous or don't care about our customers," I said.

"No one thinks that. When tragedy strikes, people need someone to blame," Misty said.

Fran nodded. "When my husband died, my son wanted to know why I was out shopping. Why I hadn't been home to call for an ambulance."

"That's awful. I know people in grief say and do awful things, but I just wanted to make sure that no one here saw any signs of illness. Or thought there was any foul play from any direction. I know Martha had health issues, and the police seem to think that was the cause, but I didn't know her very well. A few minutes a day doesn't give much insight. Martha wasn't chatty," I said.

"No, she didn't disclose a lot of personal stuff to strangers. But she liked your place more than the chains. She thought you needed more flowers," Joyce said.

"Oh, she never said that to me. It could cheer things up. Especially with this weather. Do you guys have indoor gardens?" I asked.

"We work on herbs and potted plants in the winter. We also plan our summer gardens. If you want to win, you need to be creative." Fran nodded.

"Win? Did Martha win a lot?" I asked.

"She did. But no one would hurt her over that," Sara said with a chuckle.

"Right. Her question. No one we know wanted to hurt Martha or had a problem with her. She had a happy marriage. Her daughter was happily married with a grandson. Martha doted on him. She loved her work. She'd been a member of this club for two decades. Her flowers ended up in her church regularly. She made up baskets for funerals and such, as well. I can't imagine anyone wanting to hurt her." Joyce shrugged.

"Did she have a problem with the witch theme of our shop?" I asked.

Misty shifted in her chair. "She wasn't a fan, but at one point, we talked about the history of the town. She complained there were so many witch-themed places. I'm a history teacher at the high school, and a lot of people don't know about our history because Salem steals all the thunder and tourists."

"Thanks for educating people," I said.

"Do you want to stay for the meeting or do you have what you need?" Fran looked sharply at the clock on the wall.

"I think that's it, unless anyone has anything else that they think I should know or want to share." I felt like I was getting politely tossed out.

No one else spoke so I stood. At that moment, I realized how useful a card would be. The police had them, and Bran had them. I should order some.

"Well, thank you. Have a nice meeting. I'm going to hit the restroom and brave the snow." I felt like I was babbling. It was uncomfortable, but I had sort of crashed their meeting without notice, and that wasn't very fair.

I found the ladies room and used it. As I washed my hands, I noticed the door open. It was Sara.

Pick Your Potion

"Sorry if they were rude. Those women have a schedule, and it never changes. Year in and year out. Month in and month out. They care about Martha, but some probably thought you were accusing them," she said.

I dried my hands with paper towels and nodded. "Sorry, I should have called ahead or something. I get the feeling there is more to this than I know, and people are blaming me."

"Mr. O'Conner is ruining your business. And people aren't telling you everything. But we can't talk here." She handed me a card. "Call me after five, and we'll set up something."

"Thanks," I said.

"I have to get back." She slipped out.

I touched up my lipstick and put moisturizer on my hands before I left, so it wasn't obvious Sara and I had been chatting. I got the feeling the people around here were regulars and noticed other people's patterns a lot. Back to the cold weather. I had some phone calls to make and business cards to order.

Chapter Fifteen

I called, and Sara was happy to stop by the coffee shop. Since I'd never seen any of the other ladies in my shop, I didn't think it would matter. Filling the biggest cup we had with tea, I tried to figure out what secrets the garden club had. The Wiccan meetings also had me itching to find out more, but I had to prioritize.

"Mr. O'Conner didn't show?" I asked my aunt, hoping that Mrs. Reynolds had worked her magic.

"Oh, no, he did. We called the cops." She sighed.

Sara walked in and gave me a quick smile. She ordered a lemon tea, and I gestured her to join me.

We went into my office because there were too many people who'd get nosy if I just went to my table. My aunt would come over and introduce herself at the very least.

"Please sit," I said.

"Sorry I couldn't just tell you earlier. Those women are sharks. They gossip like crazy about others, but if you tell anything about them, even the truth, they go on the attack." She set her tea on my desk then pulled off her gloves.

"It's fine. I hope this won't get you in trouble with the other ladies. I'm only looking for info that would really throw suspicion on someone hurting Martha," I said.

Pick Your Potion

"That's just it. I don't think they'd actually kill her. But I know they lied to the police." She sipped her tea.

"Who lied?" I asked.

"Fran. The president of the club. She said she had no issues with Martha. They were like sisters. Always got along great. Old friends." Sara rolled her eyes.

"It's not true? Martha wanted to be president?" I asked.

"I'm sure she did, but Martha wasn't nice enough to people to be voted in. She thought her stuff was better. She was overly competitive and critical. It's about enjoying flowers and helping each other, not a war to see who has the best garden. Fran had to handle Martha when she got too snippy. But they have some older issues, as well. They were never really friends. More like frenemies," she said.

"That sounds like everyone Martha knew. Not really a motive for murder, though," I said.

"No, not that part. Fran got a divorce about seven years ago. Her husband found her with Mr. O'Conner. It was insane. I mean, he seemed like such a devoted husband. Martha was always sort of the dominant one. There were fights. And canceled meetings. But Martha insisted they wouldn't divorce like Fran. She never missed a meeting. She didn't run against Fran for president after that. It was tense and weird. It all sort of calmed down eventually, and no one talked about it for years. But Martha held a grudge. Fran did, too. There used to be twenty people in the group,

144

but with their tension and occasional dustups, the people left." Sara shook her head.

"You think Fran is still interested in Mr. O'Conner?" I asked.

"I don't know about that, but quality senior men are hard to find. Maybe they kept up a connection. I don't know. I have no idea when she'd have had the chance to hurt Martha. I mean, we were all in the room together for that meeting. She was fine when she left. It's probably nothing," she said.

"Maybe. But I appreciate your honesty. I know they have the tox screen back with no results. So, I'm guessing it wasn't a plant," I replied.

"There are some lethal plants. But with Martha's health issues, it'd be much easier to kill that way," Sara said casually.

"I'm sorry?" I asked.

"Oh, sorry, I'm a nurse. Martha could've been given a huge dose of sugar water. Or too much insulin. Either would kill her. She was on high blood pressure meds. Beta blockers. If someone swapped out those pills, her heart would be under more strain. All of those wouldn't show up in a tox screen." Sara waved it off.

"That's scary. They wouldn't check for sugar?" I asked.

"Not unless the ME specifically ordered a glucose test. Insulin is naturally occurring in your body. So is sugar. You'd have to test for a level. I think she was on a sleeping pill, too. That could've done it."

"A sleeping pill?" I asked.

145

Pick Your Potion

"Well, some people take more than one. If you take too many, that's a problem. Or she could miss taking her insulin or eating if she sleeps too long, then slip into a coma. As brittle as she is, her body would start to shut down. We had her in for kidney trouble once at the hospital. All the meds and everything takes a toll on the liver and kidneys that process them. She was so lucky she wasn't on permanent dialysis. That's where she was heading."

I stared at her tea.

"I'm sorry; I'm not supposed to share her medical details. You knew about the diabetes. But I could get fired." She fidgeted in her chair.

"It's fine. I won't say anything. I appreciate your help, but it was all hypothetical. I swear, no one will hear any of it from me," I said.

"I never do that. I didn't mean to tell that." She frowned.

"It's okay. You care about her. I wouldn't be running around town, trying to find out things if I didn't. The privacy stuff in this world has gotten out of control. But I know you have to respect it because it's your job." I wouldn't get anyone in trouble.

"I should go," she said.

"Thanks for coming." I walked her out then turned to find my aunt.

"Good talk?" she asked.

"Did you spike her drink with a truth potion?" I asked.

Aunt Mandy frowned at me. "Esmeralda did. I assume it was useful?" she asked.

146

I shrugged. "Yes and no. Nothing is simple about this," I said.

"We haven't found out who threatened Mrs. O'Conner, yet. We must have a rogue witch. Esme is trying to scout that angle while you're doing this," she said.

"You think I should stop and be more with the coven?" I asked.

She leaned in. "Pushing the issue for proof on Mrs. O'Conner only makes it look like you're afraid of being accused. Or afraid someone here did it."

"So, I should let it go?" I asked.

"I know you're trying to help to keep this business going, but the customers are getting used to Mr. O'Conner. The slow down isn't as bad, anymore."

"As bad?" I asked. "It's still fewer people every day. When he's out there, it gets really quiet in here. We need closure."

"Only the autopsy will give you that. And the police's work. You're not the police. You're not a private investigator," she said.

"I know, but I need to be sure a murderer isn't getting away. What if they rule natural causes? We know it's not," I said.

She looked down.

"What? Let it go?" I asked.

"The spell could be wrong. Maybe she did it to herself?" my aunt asked.

"Suicide? No note?" I asked.

She shrugged. "You don't know. A false conviction would be worse."

"Thanks for the advice. I have to go," I said.

Pick Your Potion

"Make kind choices," she said.

I tracked down Fran. Apparently, she worked evenings at a flower shop. She stared daggers at me when I walked in.

"Do you have a minute to talk?" I asked.

She nodded and led me to the back of the shop where she worked on creating some very pretty bouquets.

"I'm sorry to bother you here," I said.

"Are you?" she asked.

"I just found out some information, and I wanted to ask you about it," I said.

"I didn't do anything to Martha. I'm sure someone told you about the affair. It was years ago," she replied.

"Why didn't you just tell me, then?" I asked.

"It's not your business. It's history."

I suddenly wished I'd taken an allergy pill. My nose didn't like one of the pollens back there.

I sneezed.

"Bless you. You didn't seem like a flowers girl," she said.

"Thanks. Fresh flowers could trigger allergies for customers, so we don't have them. I knew there was a reason." I sniffed. "But, obviously, you know a side of the O'Conner family others don't. You were involved with Mr. O'Conner. Are you still involved?" I asked.

"No. Not for years. Marriage is a long and complicated business. Things aren't always good. You're too young to understand that. But it's true. You can love someone, but all the spark and the passion are gone after kids and years of taking care of them. I ruined my marriage over feeling wanted. My ex had his wounded pride. Now, he's in a home with dementia. That's what he gets for that." She stabbed a rose into a vase.

That was cold, and she still took it very personally.

"But Martha forgave her husband?" I asked.

"She did. Sort of. She didn't want the embarrassment of divorce. There was a time when people stayed together 'til death. They only had one child and one grandchild. They didn't want to stress out the family and cause pain. He felt very guilty and didn't want to upset her health. I doubt he'd stray, again. But there are plenty of women interested. He's a good-looking man for his age with a good pension."

"So, you don't know anyone else he's cheated with?" I asked.

"No. And I didn't hurt Martha. Maybe she goofed up her meds. She was always complaining about how the mail order place was changing what generics they sent her because their medical covered the cheapest stuff. And calling them only made her angrier. I think you're looking for a smoking gun and maybe she just was getting confused. It happens." She shrugged.

"Right. Okay. Thanks for your time." I rubbed my nose, trying not to sneeze again.

"No man is worth killing over," Fran said, half to me and half to herself.

"I agree," I muttered to myself.

I left the flower shop and sneezed a few more times. My aunt was big into flowers, but clearly there was a flower out there that didn't like me.

Pick Your Potion

Another dead end for the murder investigation. I needed some tea and a hot bath.

Chapter Sixteen

I couldn't refuse a family dinner request from my aunt. She did make the best pasta and garlic bread. Being back in the home I grew up in made me feel safe. My brain buzzed with suspects and what-ifs. The twins were helping their mom in the kitchen as I sipped tea and set the salad on the table.

Uncle Vinny walked up as the girls brought out the pasta. We sat and began dishing out the food.

"That hunter is a real handful in the basement. He's all better. When is he leaving?" Violet asked.

"I thought you guys liked that flirty pain in the neck," I teased.

Iris rolled her eyes. "He's always asking us to get him things. Or help him leave. It's weird. He's hot, but something is off."

I shot my uncle a look.

"It's cabin fever. Hunters don't like to be cooped up," he replied.

"Isn't he safe here?" my aunt asked.

My uncle sighed. "He is. He probably wants to get back to work. Check on some friends and family. That's why it's better to hold him longer. The police might be watching his friends and family. He can sit tight, for now."

"I'd still like more details on the case he was involved in," I said.

Pick Your Potion

"We couldn't find much," Violet said.

"What about Mrs. O'Conner's case?" Iris asked.

I sighed. "I've talked to almost everyone she met with that day. She was fine. She had some enemies, but I don't see how they had opportunity. The tox screen found nothing. So, if it wasn't a poison that struck her down later...maybe it was natural causes?"

"You think your spell was wrong?" my aunt asked.

"I chose my words carefully, but maybe I missed something. Some other option. Or maybe it was a combination of things? If her health was really bad, then one thing could trip it, and her heart gave out. We're waiting on the autopsy, but I feel like I'm missing something." I took a bite of garlic bread and chewed it while looking for that missing piece in the case.

"I agree with Esmeralda. It's not your job. If you keep meddling in police work, you'll only get more attention," Uncle Vinny said.

I stabbed my pasta with my fork and twirled. "She was threatened for threatening the witches. Maybe that's the lead I need to follow. Who made those threats?"

"Someone calling and threatening isn't likely a murderer. It's like on Snapchat. People are so cruel to each other, but most people wouldn't actually do any of the things they threaten," Violet said.

"Threaten. Who's threatened you?" I asked.

Uncle Vinny sat up straighter, as well.

"No, nothing specific," Vi backtracked.

"Don't lie to me," my aunt shot at her daughter.

"I'm in a few pagan groups, and one girl mocks those of us without powers. We're just pretend witches. I blocked her." Violet shrugged it off.

"So, no one you know personally? No one from school or the coven?" I asked.

Iris and Violet exchanged a look.

"Spill it," Uncle Vinny said.

"We sort of kept in touch with Katrina and Lily. They left their freshman year of high school when we were sophomores, but we stayed friends on social media," Iris admitted.

"They're your cousins. That's not bad." My aunt nodded.

"Well, now, they're sixteen, and both are getting married. Married. They're bragging about their rings and dresses. At first, it was bridezilla stuff but normal. Then, they started making fun of us for going to college. We're alone and going to school while they'll be married with their own homes and everything." Violet shoved a forkful of salad in her mouth and chewed with a vengeance.

"That's crazy. You're not gypsies. Don't compare your lifestyle to theirs," I said.

"Exactly, you're not getting married until you're done with college. I have nothing against homemakers or stay-at-home moms, but men don't always stick around, and you need to be able to take care of yourself," my aunt said.

"Gypsy men stick around. But that's not the life I want for you. Block those girls," Vinny ordered.

Pick Your Potion

"But they're our cousins. Your nieces," Iris said.

"We sort of grew up with them," Vi agreed.

"You don't need them if they aren't respecting your life choices. You haven't attacked theirs," my aunt insisted.

"I get it," I said softly.

"You do?" Vinny asked.

I nodded. "I don't have siblings. I couldn't cut you guys off if you went full-on gypsy. I'd miss you guys. Family is important. The less you have, the more you see it. Just ignore their attitude and be happy they're happy. You define happy differently. When your weddings come along, you'll be the star of the show, and nothing will be more important. You won't rub it in anyone else's faces, but your single friends still might feel a little jealous. Just think long term. The wedding is one day. Then, they're wives. They'll have a bunch of kids and be tied down to cooking and cleaning for the next twenty years."

The twins smiled.

"They'll have stretch marks before they're twenty," Iris said.

"Kindness," my aunt said.

"So, are we invited to the wedding?" I asked.

Vinny shrugged. "They are my nieces. Yes. But we don't have to go."

They gypsies hadn't really accepted my aunt or the twins because they didn't adopt the gypsy lifestyle. We'd been to a few weddings and parties for gypsy relations, depending on how close Uncle Vin was with them. I couldn't believe he'd snub his own nieces.

CC Dragon

"I don't have to go. I know I don't really belong, but you guys should go," I said.

"I could always have to work," my aunt offered.

"No, we all should go. Claudia, bring a date. It'll make them crazy," Violet said with a grin.

"You bring a date," I said.

"That would look bad. Disrespectful," Vinny said.

I rolled my eyes.

"Vi and Iris are my daughters. If I let them run wild, I'm a bad father. You're my niece and a Gorger. You have no gypsy blood, at all. You can bring a date," Vin replied.

"What's with the dating push? Esme is nagging. Now, you guys?" I asked.

"You are obsessing about Mrs. O'Conner. And your life is all about the coffee shop. You need a life," Violet said.

"I have a life. The coven and the coffee shop are all that matter. I have a hunter in the basement. I have a dead customer. That's a lot." I pushed pasta around my plate.

My aunt refilled our glasses of iced tea. "You need a love life. Esme said there is a nice and very strong wizard in that Killean family."

"They're recluses. I heard they're all ugly," Iris said.

"That's not true. Crazy old rumors," I replied.

My aunt and the twins shared a smile. I'd walked into that one.

"You've met him?" Vin asked.

"He came into the coffee shop. Apparently, he keeps vampire hours. He was nice but a bit full of

155

Pick Your Potion

himself. What does Esme know about him, anyway?" I asked.

"She's been doing some private classes for some new or young witches. The coven classes are for everyone, powerful or not. She has some other clients," my aunt said.

"Why didn't she tell me that?" I asked.

"You have enough on your plate. You don't need to do private tutoring. Your skills are still developing." My aunt began clearing plates.

I helped her and felt better alone in the kitchen.

"Am I ignoring something?" I asked her.

"You've always had your own path and gifts. I never would've imagined you'd use the money your mother left you to open a coffee shop. If you want to follow this death case, there is a reason. You don't want to neglect your personal happiness either." She dished out a hot pan of brownies. "I know you're afraid."

I grabbed the vanilla bean ice cream from the freezer, then the scoop from the drawer. "Afraid?"

"You lost your parents young. You were loved, but you're afraid of letting more people in because they could hurt you. As long as you have those walls up, your power can't expand, and you won't really be happy. The twins can't understand, but I do. I lost my sister." She pinched my cheek.

"I can't rush into a relationship because you and Esme like some guy's powers," I said.

She nodded. "I'm not pushing you toward anyone. But he would understand your life more than a human man. You wouldn't like a hunter either. Certainly not a gypsy."

156

"You're right." I followed her out into the dining room, and we served dessert.

As I entered the coffee shop, I was still thinking about how well my aunt knew me. A man without powers or gifts would bore me. A gypsy would make me want to argue gender roles. A hunter would make me question every kill he made. My dating pool of interesting men was extremely small.

Was I really that narrow-minded? A human might be interesting enough. I liked humans. There were plenty in my coven without powers.

Esme was coming up from the basement as I was passing through the main area.

"How was dinner?" she asked.

"Fine. You should've come," I said. Aunt Mandy always invited Esme and tried to make her feel like family. She was distantly a cousin of my mother and aunt.

"No, I'm a loner by nature. I did have a word with that hunter. He keeps trying to use the phones and get out. I've put a magical perimeter up for the night," she said.

"Thanks. So, are you giving private lessons to a Killean? Is that why you want me to go out with Bran?" I asked.

She smiled. "Bran?"

"I've met him. My aunt mentioned your private lessons. Does Bran have a sister?" I asked.

"No, he has a younger brother, but he doesn't need my help. They have a cousin staying with them, now. Her parents are traveling in Europe, and she wanted to try the college thing. She's

Pick Your Potion

nineteen but a freshman. She took a year off. Her magic needs work. She has powers, but her parents thought everything she did was perfect and didn't really push her."

"The way you pushed me?" I teased her.

"Exactly. She needs work, but her ego is so fragile." Esme sighed.

"That's a shame. There's always more to learn and always someone stronger, so ego is a bad thing to get wrapped up in." I was taught young that hard work and intention mattered. If I let my powers go to my head, a stronger witch would put me in my place. There was a pecking order and rules to the witching world.

"How's your human death case, Nancy Drew?" Esme asked.

I laughed. "I always liked a good mystery. But I'm stuck. No one with motive had access. They weren't in her home that night. There was nothing found on the tox, so it had to be done fairly quickly to her. Maybe my spell was wrong?"

Esme frowned. "I don't think so. The light left the room. Someone out there has some culpability but it might not be in the way you think. It may be beyond someone actually murdering her. She could've been driven to it. Something could've been planted or messed with in her home. I still wish I knew who threatened Mrs. O'Conner. We need to keep order or things will get worse."

"Worse?" I asked.

"At times, humans think they must root us out. Protest and convert us. They fear us. Then, there are times when the witches feel they are stronger and they should teach humans a lesson about history and crossing people with more powers. Right now, it feels like both sides are posturing for a fight. Conservatives taking over the country. But supernatural forces are aligning. Our powers are stronger. You are vulnerable and incredibly important."

"That's why you want me married to a powerful wizard? Backup?" I asked.

"I'm not pushing you to do anything as serious as marriage. But networking with the powerful wouldn't hurt you. You look too sympathetic to humans. People understand because of your parents and who ended up raising you. But they want you to understand who you are. Who your mother was. What your true potential is. Spending time with the Killean brothers would help. The younger one is currently studying vampires in Romania, but he'll be back in a month or so. You might like him better. He's the same age as you and more adventurous. Bran can be a real homebody." Esme shrugged.

"How do I socialize with them? I mean, I have a coven," I said.

"Old witch and wizard families don't join covens. They don't need to. They throw parties, meet at certain clubs, and network among their own kind. I'll bring you along next time. You're ready. I didn't want to upset you before," she replied.

"Upset me? Sounds like these people are more like me." I smiled.

"Yes and no. They were raised with magic to an extreme. They wouldn't marry a human or do

Pick Your Potion

things the human way. You probably washed the dishes at your aunt's house by hand," she said.

I shook my head. "It was the twins' turn. I see what you mean, though. I'll feel like I'm behind. I already do. I should've been able to use those spells and find the killer."

"Human and paranormal worlds converging makes things much trickier. We'll open an inquiry into the threats to Mrs. O'Conner. That might help rule out witches or wizards. But it might be a human customer or Wiccan coven member who did it. Threats are easy. That would be a very human thing to do," she said.

"You're right. But if we can find out who did that, I'll feel a little better. Some answers. I still need to talk to the grandson." I was dreading it. The kid's online presence was smug and rotten.

"You think a kid killed his grandmother? That's a long shot. Even with a human. But stranger things have happened, I suppose."

I picked out a tea bag. I needed something to warm me up. "Even if he noticed anything about her feeling ill at dinner. I could try talking to Mr. O'Conner, but he's our resident protester. He probably won't say a word."

She poured us two cups of hot water, and we dunked our tea bags. "Can't hurt to talk to anyone, but minors are tricky. That can you get you into trouble. Now, let's talk about how to figure out who threatened Mrs. O'Conner…"

Chapter Seventeen

I staked out the library and hoped Harry Stevens would follow his routine. With his grandmother's death, anything was possible. Esme was right. Bothering minors was probably a bad idea. The kid had, no doubt, been instructed not to talk to anyone, like the rest of his family. But his social media proved he was easily baited. He complained about his interfering family and being diabetic. I mentioned to the librarian that I was looking for him, so hopefully she'd help me out.

I browsed the sections on witch history, which was bigger than most since the history was local and true.

"You're that coffee lady," a young guy behind me said.

I turned and saw the kid I was after. "True. You've been in my shop." He had been in with a bunch of his friends. Kids always wanted to act older. I hit him with a curiosity spell, so he'd keep talking.

"Yep. I like the frozen drinks better. Too cold, now. Then again, you pissed off my grandma. Grandpa is still mad. I know you talked to my mom," he said.

"And you're okay talking to me?" I asked.

He shook his head. "Grandma was a pain. Don't blame yourself. But I don't know anything."

Pick Your Potion

"You had dinner with her that night. She seemed fine?" I asked.

He nodded. "Nagging and complaining, as always. She wanted me to get an insulin pump because I kept forgetting my shots. It's not like I'm a baby. I'm not disabled."

"Hardly. There are much worse things to have. Some kids have cancer. Managing that isn't really in anyone's control." I shrugged.

He gave me a funny look. "So, I should be grateful I don't have a worse disease? You sound just like Grandma."

"Should I be flattered or insulted?" I chuckled. "She just wanted you healthy. When grownups can't control things, it makes them crazy. My aunt still insists on brewing me this anti-stress tea, at times. Whether I want it or not."

"Why do you let her? You could just pick up and move away. Not be nagged," he said.

"My parents died when I was little. She's all I've got in the mom department. And when I am sick or stressed, it's nice that someone cares. So, you don't want the insulin pump?" I wanted to get him talking and relaxed. Maybe he'd let something slip.

"Do you think I want guys seeing that when I change for gym? I want to play sports, too. Girls don't think about the locker room. That thing makes me look like a wimp. Plus, everything I do has to go through the doctor. My mom is fussy enough. How did I get Type 1, and my mom didn't, but Grandma had it? How is that fair?"

I shook my head. "Not fair. Life sucks, at times. Like, now, you'll have to go to a funeral. I promise, one day you'll miss your grandma's nagging. Maybe not for a long time, but you will. I just wish I knew how convince your grandfather I had nothing to do with it. My coffee shop isn't behind something."

"Yeah. Mom said there was nothing on the tox screen. You'd think that'd be enough. Grandma had a lot of meds and issues. Until the final guy signs off and says what killed her, Grandpa won't believe anything else. Sorry."

The kid was less of a jerk than I thought. Certainly less cocky than he came off on social media.

"Thanks. At least not everyone in your family thinks my shop is evil." I smiled.

"My mom brews her own coffee at home and thinks buying fancy coffee is overpriced, but she doesn't think your place sucks."

"Thanks. Well, I'm sorry about your grandma. I hope the police determine the cause, and everyone can move on. It just seems odd that she was fine all day long and then suddenly died. But I guess that's life and death." I shrugged.

He nodded. "She did get confused, sometimes."

"Confused?" I asked.

He frowned. "Not like Alzheimer's confused. She always knew who we were and who she was. She took a sleeping pill, and sometimes, she'd forget what time it was and call at two in the morning. Or go online and buy shoes. Or make a bunch of cookies and eat them. She never remembered it. Grandpa had to check her blood sugar and everything to be safe. The docs tried to

Pick Your Potion

get her off that sleeping pill, but the insomnia was worse. Now, if you're so smart, tell me how to avoid this damn insulin pump."

I shifted my weight to one leg and propped a hand on my hip. "The best way to get adults to back off is show you can handle it the way it is. Test your blood on a routine, eat right, and take the shots on time and all that crap without complaint or slip up. All your mom cares about is your health. If doing it that way is too much of a hassle, you might decide the pump would be better. The other kids probably already know you're diabetic if you're testing and injecting. More kids will know, and girls talk. The pump might actually cut down on it. I'd look at both sides and decide what's best for your social life."

He half-smiled. "I didn't think about that. People do notice at lunch and stuff."

"And if you're on a team? I don't know how that all works, but sometimes, practices go long or there are tournament days when you play a few games. It could be safer with a pump regulating you instead of risking it. If you want to be a jock, less dependence on the testing and injections can't hurt." I smiled.

He stared at me for a second as though rolling over my advice in his head. "Maybe you're right. My mom would fuss less, which helps. Thanks. I have to get going." He headed down the aisle of books.

The kid was about image. He wouldn't hurt someone, but he resented his grandmother for sharing the disease. Maybe I was chasing crazy leads.

Mr. O'Conner was outside the café, again, protesting. I cast a warming spell on him. Truthfully, he wasn't making much of a dent in our customer base, anymore. We'd put notices out on social media, explaining the situation. Most of our customers came back, yet this man persisted.

I watched him from inside.

"Want me to call the police?" Esme asked.

"No. Let him learn we won't play his game, anymore." I removed the warming spell. "He can go home or stay. No more babying him. He may be grieving, but he can't keep blaming us. The results will be in soon enough, and we can all move on."

"No luck with the grandson?" she asked.

"He didn't do it and knows nothing. He mentioned she takes a lot of meds. It might be natural. Find any suspects for the threats?" I asked.

"Not really. Some solo witches may have heard about the insult. They sometimes come in here. But there's no way to prove it. It'd just be questioning people. They'd all deny it and resent us for doubting them. We need more proof or a confession before we accuse anyone. Your reputation has taken enough of a hit. I'll ask around to my connections, but I don't want to look like we're on a witch hunt. I know it was my idea, but we can't go about it the way you're chasing down humans like they're suspects. We have to be more subtle," she said.

"Unless they were here, they'd have to have heard it from someone who was. Ugh. I don't want

165

Pick Your Potion

to think about this, anymore. I feel like I've followed every logical angle and found nothing. Maybe it is all nothing. Natural causes and some hollow threats. I'm worried for nothing. Or I missed something." I sank into a chair.

"You need to forget about it for a bit. You're obsessed, and your mind needs a break. Come back at it with fresh eyes. Go to bed and get some rest. Watch some mindless TV or read a book. Get yourself away from this stuff." She nodded.

"You're right. I'm going to go to the movies. Not be here for a bit," I said.

"Sounds like a plan. Go. I'll cover for you here," she said.

"Thanks." I needed a mental break. The only decisions I needed to make were what to see, how big of a popcorn to buy and what flavor to add to my diet soda.

Chapter Eighteen

The movie was okay, but the time outside of my own head had worked. I felt refreshed and somehow like I'd hit the reset button on my brain. I didn't have all the answers, but I was clearer on some things. I'd wait for the human report and see how they would handle it. Redo my spells and, if it was murder, pursue the guilty party with paranormal justice.

I waved to Brad and headed upstairs to my room. I wasn't alone. A man was bent over my nightstand, using my phone.

Magically, I spun him around. The phone fell to the floor.

Ryan.

"Didn't Esme lock you up tonight?" I asked.

"No, I think she forgot." He gave me that flirty grin.

"What are you doing here? Stealing? Using my phone?"

"Who has a landline, anymore?" he teased.

"It's for the security system. And spam calls. What did you do? Why are you trying to get away so badly?" I challenged him.

"What did I do? I killed a werewolf who was killing humans. By our laws, it's fine. All the humans see is a human body, and that's bad. Even if it's collateral damage in my job, no one understands. I want to move on. Farther away.

Pick Your Potion

But I need to check on my sister. You don't seem to care," he said.

"You chose your job, and you're the one who has to manage your family and work. I've got my own problems." I pushed him out of my bedroom. "Wait. Collateral damage?"

"You do have your own problems. Someone was snooping down in your storeroom. I came up here to avoid being caught down there. You don't want people to know I'm here, right?" he asked.

"Define people." I magically flung him down the stairs.

"Damn, is that necessary?" he asked.

I stepped over him and walked to the counter. "You let him upstairs?" I asked Brad.

"Um, he got spooked by Belle. The other baristas are helping her stock, so he can go back. I told him to wait in the sitting area on the second floor while I had some customers. Not to go into your private room."

"Well, he doesn't listen." I turned when I heard the bell on the door.

Bran walked in. Perfect timing. Why did that man always show up when I had chaos on my hands?

"Bad time?" Bran asked.

"Horrid, actually." I smiled. I magically pushed Ryan toward the basement as Belle came up the stairs.

"Sorry," she said.

"No, it's not you. It's our ever-rude guest." I pointed to Ryan. "Jail."

He disappeared. Once I felt him there, I went further. "Locked."

CC Dragon

"Impressive," Bran said.

I laughed. "Not really. I grew up with twins who were always changing places. I learned teleportation young, so I wasn't caught up in their tricks. They tried to blame me."

"I can't believe that. Iris and Violet are too sweet," Belle said.

"Kids are never perfectly sweet. We all test the rules growing up. Belle Andrews, Bran Killean. Belle is a gypsy witch who supplies us with expired blood from the blood bank to keep our vampires fed safely. Bran is..." I paused.

"I've heard of his family." Belle blushed a bit and shook his hand. "Never thought I'd meet one."

"A gypsy? Forgive me, I thought the women stayed at home. You're a modern gypsy?" Bran asked.

"I guess." Belle tugged her coat tight around her. She was cute and sweet but thirty, and in gypsy years, that was an old maid.

"Belle chose a career. I think it was a better choice than getting married at sixteen," I said.

"I'd tend to agree with you, but I don't want to seem anti-gypsy traditions. My family takes its share of judgment. I don't want others to think I disapprove. We all have to do what works for us." Bran smiled at me and Belle.

The man was a flirt. Or he was this attentive and nice to every woman? Maybe I should wait for the brother to come home? I didn't really know either of them well.

"I'd better go. Mom always waits up. Nice meeting you," Belle said to Bran. "Bye, Claudia."

169

Pick Your Potion

"Bye, thanks. Sorry about Ryan. The vampires were supposed to keep a handle on him." I shot Brad a look.

The other barista came up from the basement. "Blood is stocked."

"Good. Hopefully, by the next delivery, Ryan will be gone," I said.

"Great. Are you coming to the wedding?" Belle asked as she lingered at the door.

"Probably. See you there?"

She nodded. "Mom insists. Gotta go."

I waved. "Say hi to your mom for me."

Bran remained quiet until she left.

"Complicated culture?" he asked.

"Yes. But I'm just a guest. Belle and her sister wanted more than to be housewives." I knew more about the details of her family life that explained a lot, but Bran didn't need to know.

"Quite the rebels. And you're invited to a wedding?' he asked.

"My uncle is a gypsy. It's his nieces getting married. Double wedding. We're not the most popular family to go, but my aunt and uncle don't believe in cutting off family ties if they can help it. Sorry, I should go check on my horrible guest," I said.

"Your troubles tend to linger," he said.

I shrugged. "I can't force the human world to work faster."

"Want some help putting him in his place?" Bran offered.

"I can handle it." I headed down the stairs, feeling like I should invite him, but it wasn't his business or his problem.

170

Ryan paced in his cage. "You need to let me go. Just kick me out. You'll never see me again."

"If I believed that, I'd do it so fast your head would spin. I think you'll run back here. I don't need more headaches. Who were you calling?" I demanded.

"Does it matter? You lock me up. Cut me off from my family and friends. You hold me hostage. I could call the police," he said.

I laughed. "I'm protecting you from the police. Please do call them. I'll hand you over, at this point. My uncle will get over it."

"I need to get out of here," he insisted.

"Why? Did you kill Mrs. O'Conner? Did you think it was a favor or something?" I asked.

"No, I didn't kill her. I was beat up here that night. I couldn't even have made those threats."

"You know about those?" I asked.

"Esme vents. She thinks I don't listen. She talks to herself, sometimes. Who knows what she might've said to someone about that annoying old woman before? The threats might not even be related to the murder," he said.

"You've spent a lot of time thinking about that, have you?" I asked.

"What else do I have to do here? Oh, you're stocking too much eggnog. People don't seem to like it in their coffee. But I'd make a shake out of it," he said.

"The holidays are over, anyway," I said.

"I'd keep a minty green shake year-round. People like it. Maybe do holiday flavors in July. When it's hot and people want something cold

Pick Your Potion

and delicious. Peppermint and all those flavors."
He shrugged.

It wasn't a horrible idea. "Thanks. Now, back
to the real question. Why are you trying to blame
Esme?"

"I'm not blaming her. She just talks a lot.
Someone out there might've threatened the old
woman to curry favor with you. Or even killed her
to please you when they heard about her threats.
You don't know how powerful and known you
are," he said.

"Flattery crap won't work," I said.

"That part is true," said a voice behind me.

Bran had followed me.

"What are you doing, spying on me? Nosing
around my property?" I asked.

"I just want to help if I can. Esme asked if I
could try and get you involved more in our world.
Your powers are known and still growing." Bran
nodded.

"Esme is more powerful," I said.

"Barely, and she's a century older than you.
You like humans, and that's nice, but you need to
grow you powers and flex them." Bran glared at
Ryan. "This human is not worth your time."

"You're a stronger wizard than I am a witch.
Why do you want the competition?" I asked.

He smiled. "Competition makes us stronger.
You let your guard down because you're on top.
It's good to be pushed. Challenge me."

"Do I need to be here for this?" Ryan asked.

"I can take him off your hands for you. I
promise he'll never escape my dungeons," Bran
said.

"Not cool, dude," Ryan said.

"Thanks for the offer, but I'll handle my own problems." I added a magical perimeter until morning then walked up the stairs.

Bran followed me.

"I don't think I helped," Bran said.

"Actually, you gave me some information that helps. Esme put you up to this. Chatting with me. Helping me. It makes sense, now," I said.

"No," he said firmly.

"Yes. I'm not a fool. I appreciate any help to socialize with the witching world. I don't know why it's such a big deal. My aunt never pushed me. Esme never did either before. What's changed?" I asked.

Bran shook his head. "I'm not sure. I know, when your mother died, it was big news in the magical and paranormal community. She was such a strong witch. Esme promised to make sure you were connected, but your aunt kept you from the groups and activities as a child."

"You were included in them?" I asked.

"No, but that's my family. You don't cultivate a certain reputation by joining in everything. I knew about them. We occasionally were allowed to do something over the summer. My brother pushed for it more than I." Bran folded his arms.

"You have a brother?" I asked.

"Esme didn't tell you?" he replied.

I played disinterested rather than dumb. "She mentioned someone in Romania studying and also you have a cousin staying. I didn't retain all the details. Human trouble."

Pick Your Potion

"My brother is studying the history of vampires. Myths and facts. He'd love to meet your gypsy blood fairy. My cousin is staying. She wanted to try college but needs Esme's magical tutoring. Her skills are lacking. Her parents let her run a bit wild and free with humans. We should really go back to boarding schools."

"Like Hogwarts?" I laughed.

"Don't mock it. Homeschooling and private tutors only works so well. Trying to fit into a human world makes us weak and fearful of them. We need to organize and be stronger." He looked me dead in the eye.

"I agree there. But we can't ignore humans. We need to know what they're thinking and planning. Anyway, I'm sure Esme will help your cousin. When your brother comes back, please bring him by. I'd love to meet him, and Belle would, too." I smiled.

"Why don't we get to know each other better before that?" he asked.

"You don't have to do anything special with me. Esme put you up to it, and it's not needed," I said.

"Dinner can't hurt. Fill in some blanks about things. Then, I can escort you to the Vernal Equinox ball. My cousin says I need to get a life," he said with a smirk.

"I'm hearing that a lot. We can blame Esme for that nugget being planted, I'm sure." I chuckled.

"Doesn't mean we can't be good allies and friends—if not more. Our dating pool isn't as massive as humans have. You might like my brother better. I couldn't let him marry a gypsy, anyway," Bran said.

"Let him?" I asked.

"Strong magical families have to keep their powers strong. Bring in power, not eccentricity."

"You're already rich and powerful," I shot back.

"Riches can be invested, built on, preserved and grown. Power, magical power, is individual. A weak wife would hurt him," Bran replied casually.

"Then, you don't know much about gypsies. Many of them have the sight. Visions of the future, and the curse of a gypsy witch is one of the hardest to break. Just because they don't socialize with your kind doesn't mean you should underestimate me or my gypsy cousins."

"You said you weren't a gypsy," he said.

"I'm not. But my uncle is, and that means I have extended family that is. I've known many of them all my life. I might not be as strong as you, but I know gypsy magic that you've never even heard of." I smiled and picked up a cup from the counter.

Brad handed Bran his coffee, as well.

"You've intrigued me. We'll have plenty to talk about over dinner. I'll pick you up Friday at seven. I wish I could help more with your human problem, but it's not my area. If you need anything, just let me know."

"Thanks. See you then. And you don't have to take me to a ball. I'm sure you have another woman you'd rather take to something that fancy." I had to wiggle out of that.

Pick Your Potion

He leaned in and smiled. "You take me to the gypsy wedding, and I'll take you to the fancy magical ball. You're fascinating, even if you want to get rid of me. You'll see at the ball that quality dating material in the witching world is very hit or miss."

"Rid of you? It depends how narrow-minded you really are. I like humans and gypsies. I just can't believe Esme put you up to this. It's not fair to ask you to give up your social life," I explained.

"I see you as more of an expansion to my social life. Until Friday." He took his coffee and left.

"Men," I grumbled.

Chapter Nineteen

The next morning, I came down to the coffee shop level to find Mr. O'Conner sitting at a table. It was barely six in the morning. He sipped a black cup of coffee. I gave Brad a look, and he just shrugged.

I walked up to our favorite protester. "Everything okay, Mr. O'Conner?" I asked.

He cleared his throat. "The police called me last night. I'm sure they'll call you, too, but I wanted to let you know I'm done. They confirmed that my wife died of natural causes. Her body just shut down. Looks like it started in her brain, but her heart gave out about the same time. They think it was a stroke. Either way, it was natural. I'm sorry I couldn't face it."

"It's all right. I've been bugging everyone in your family and all her friends to see if there were any signs. If we missed something. We'd never do anything deliberately to hurt anyone here. Whether she liked witches and pagans or not, the first rule is do no harm to anyone. I hope you believe that, now." A weight lifted off of me. The suspicion was gone. We were in the clear.

"I do. I think you need to see something, as well." He picked up three shoeboxes from the floor.

"This was her insulin and testing stuff." He opened one box.

Pick Your Potion

"This was her other meds. Heart and blood pressure. She took them religiously." He opened another full box.

"I believe you, Mr. O'Conner. I'm very sorry for all you've been through."

He nodded. "She also took a bunch of vitamins and supplements. The doctor knew about it. So many pills. But she took them. She kept active. But there are no guarantees."

"No, there aren't. Someone mentioned she took a sleeping pill. And, sometimes, it made her do things that she didn't remember later. Do you think maybe she could have forgotten she already took her meds and doubled up on something?" I asked.

"She never did that before. She'd eat or shop online. But maybe it could've happened. We'll never know, but she was a woman who wanted to live. She liked your place here. True, she complained about the witch history and pagan symbols, but our grandson loved Harry Potter when he was little. She took him to all those movies. I reminded her of that. She insisted it was different, somehow." He sat and closed the boxes.

"I think she just had to find flaws with things in her life. We couldn't be perfect," I said.

"That's true. But she liked your place better than the chains. You cared, and you have good coffee. I'm sorry I made a fuss." He sighed.

"I'm sorry if I gave you a hard time. I had to protect my reputation," I said.

He nodded. "I'm just going to finish my coffee and go meet the funeral director to make arrangements."

"If you need anything, just let Brad know," I said.

I went into my office and called Detective Shelley.

"Ah, Ms. Crestwood, I was going to call you when I got to the station."

"Oh, right. Sorry about the hour; it's a hazard of my business to be up with the early commuters. Mr. O'Conner was here and said it was all natural causes. I just needed to hear it from you guys," I said.

"It's true. Nothing toxic found in her body. Her heart and brain showed signs of system failure. The case is closed," she said with a tempered cheerfulness.

"Did they check her glucose level?" I asked.

"Why? That's not standard," she said.

I heard papers shuffling. "Well, she's a diabetic. She was on a lot of meds. I just wondered if she accidentally took too much or doubled a dose. That might explain it. But with the results in, I guess it's all done. Doesn't matter, now."

"Yep. You can move on. Any protesting issues? Mr. O'Conner seemed to take the information, and it calmed him down."

"No, no problems. He got the answers he needed. I guess I just wanted to know more. So much trouble resolved with one exam." I sighed.

"On behalf of the city, I apologize for the delay. I know it hurt your business, but we appreciate your patience. I advised Mr. O'Conner to mention in the obituary that she died of natural causes. It might help answer any customer

Pick Your Potion

questions, once and for all. Can I help you with anything else?" Shelley asked.

"No, thanks. That should help. Thank you," I said.

The human world had made their decision. Now, if they were wrong, I had to figure it out. I had to think about it and talk it through with some people.

An hour later, I invited Esme for morning coffee in the second-floor area. We sipped coffee as I told her about Mr. O'Conner and Detective Shelley. She seemed very relieved.

"So, you think my spell was wrong? That it was natural causes?" I asked.

"Oh, no, but the humans are satisfied. That's what matters first," she said.

Her face froze.

"Did you have anything to do with the threats or Mrs. O'Conner's death?" I asked.

"Certainly not."

"What aren't you telling me?" I asked.

"I have a lot of secrets. Some I can't tell you." She sat back.

The truth potion worked but I had to ask specific questions to get answers.

"Who did you tell about the threats?" I asked.

"A lot of people. I was trying to find out who did it, which means you have to talk about it. But that was after." She glared at me. "Truth potion won't last forever."

"I had to try. What secret do you know about me? What is no one telling me?" I asked.

She opened her mouth, but nothing came out. She held her throat like it was a struggle.

"Okay. Who did you see the day Mrs. O'Conner was here after her incident? Who would you have told in time to make the threats or do something?" I asked.

She shook her head. "They wouldn't."

"I remixed the potion to confirm if it was a natural death or not." I led her into the locked area on the second floor. She stared at the cauldron.

"Do it," I said.

Esme said the spell this time. Red for unnatural and green for natural causes. The potion turned pink.

"Unclear," she said.

"What do you know about me that you won't tell me? Do you know what it is?" I asked.

"I know. I can't. I swore. A bigger promise and stronger spell controls that more than your little truth potion. Move up to the big leagues." She laughed.

"Who else knows this secret?" I asked.

"Your mother," she said.

"She's dead. My aunt?" I asked.

"Yes. And uncle. One of the twins. That's all." She held up her hand.

"Why are you pushing me to engage the magical worlds, now? Why not put me in those groups and activities when I was a kid?" I pushed.

"They might have discovered your secret before."

"That would be bad?" I asked.

"It wouldn't be good." She glanced around.

Pick Your Potion

The potion might be wearing off. She was powerful enough to try and counteract it.

"Why? What is it about? My father was a gypsy?" I asked.

"No," she said flatly.

"Did I have a sibling who was killed?" I asked.

"No," she said firmly.

I was running out of ideas.

"Why is it okay for me to socialize now when I don't even know the truth? I might screw up and reveal something. Shouldn't I know?" I demanded.

"You need allies and friends like yourself. Powerful and magical. Telling you the whole truth is not my decision to make," she said.

"Which twin knows?" I asked, more as a test since I knew.

"Iris," she said.

Esme rubbed her face and walked away from the potion mix.

"That was low," she scolded.

"I needed to know if you were protecting someone. All these weird changes happening right after this death. Are you trying to distract me?" I asked.

"Please. You need a social life. You need a husband. Don't you want a powerful family?" she shot back.

"But what secret could be so bad that you kept me from socializing all of my childhood? Why can't you tell me?" I pushed.

"We had to protect you. You were gifted. I promised not to tell you." She answered the questions in order.

182

"Promised who?" I demanded.

"Your aunt." She rubbed her neck. "Enough. It's wearing off. I'm going to brew an antidote, and you better watch out that I don't mess with your memory," she warned.

"You didn't tell me enough to bother with that," I said.

"Don't go interrogating your aunt or cousins either. They won't tell," Esme said.

"What could be so bad?" I asked.

"Maybe it's not. Maybe it's good. But it's not time to tell you. It's not for me to be the one to tell you either," she replied.

"And I thought you were family. You were my mentor." I put the potion away.

Esme left the locked room before I had to throw her out. I locked the door behind us and turned to face her. "I really thought I could trust you. I never doubted you before. Now, you're keeping secrets and treating me like a child."

"It's your aunt's place to tell you. Not mine," she said.

"So, I'll go push her." I headed for the stairs.

"No, not now. Not here. That's a private conversation." She slid past me to go back to work.

The next day, I sat at my table in the café and made notes about summer promotions. Ryan's ideas weren't so terrible. I had a few for the spring. We needed to make up a bit for the dip Mr. O'Conner had caused in our winter sales. A young woman walked into the café, and I felt her power. She immediately went up to Violet and started

Pick Your Potion

chatting. The shop wasn't busy. Maybe it was a friend from school?

I kept one eye on the chatting girls. Iris joined in.

"You should really join our coven," Iris said.

"I don't know about that," the new girl said.

"You said you have powers. You should meet Claudia," Violet said.

I lifted my head. The girls looked over at me. "Come on over."

"This is a new girl at school, Serena Murray. She's very into witches and pagan stuff. She's majoring in women's studies, and the witch trials are a huge part of that," Iris said.

"How interesting. Nice to meet you, Serena." I shook her hand. "You've got powers?"

She shrugged it off sheepishly. "Sort of."

"Who are you related to? Which magical family?" I asked.

Serena went a bit pale. "Um. I'm staying with my cousins, right now. Killean."

"I know Bran. He mentioned you but not your name, so I wasn't sure. You're welcome to join our coven, but I understand if you don't want to." I sipped my tea.

"Why?" Iris asked.

"Big magical families tend to sort of be their own coven—so to speak. They don't join others where there are a lot of members without powers. The Killeans keep to themselves," I replied.

"Yeah. I'm new to the area, so I'm trying to make friends. I think the twins are great. I love this place. Great feel." Serena looked around.

184

CC Dragon

"You're welcome anytime. I have a fair set of powers myself. I've been busy with other things lately. Businesses are a lot of work," I said.

"They told me. I can't believe someone threatened this place. Rude and ignorant people really deserve to get a tough lesson," she said.

"Thanks. It's good to know there are some supporters. I'd love to hear more about your major. Maybe you could speak to our coven about the witch trials' impact on women's rights and history?" I suggested.

"Maybe, once I've had some actual classes. I took basics at a local college down in South Carolina. Then, my parents wanted to do this Euro tour thing. I wanted to keep studying. I traveled enough every summer of my childhood. I told them I'd meet up with them on summer break, but I want a degree. Bran is very supportive of that. He's always after me to do my homework and giving me magical challenges." She rolled her eyes.

"Sounds like a good atmosphere for your goals."

"You should work here," Violet said.

"Work?" Serena laughed.

"Vi, I don't think Serena needs a job. The Killeans are quite well off." I nodded.

"That's downplaying it. But, yeah, let people who need jobs take them. I need a lot of study time and magical practice," she admitted.

"Well, once you get the hang of it, you can always volunteer somewhere. If you want to give back a bit," I suggested.

185

Pick Your Potion

"Sure. Maybe a women's shelter," Serena said.

She had a theme, and I didn't hate it. "An excellent idea."

"Anyone else threatening witches?" Serena asked.

"No, that was just an annoyed customer. All cleared up," Iris said.

I leaned in. "We try not to get confrontational with our customers. Even if they're wrong. We try to educate and invite, not attack."

"Of course, do no harm," Violet said.

"Absolutely!" Serena sat. "I love the karmic balance in the world. I'd never attack anyone, but I would love to teach them about karma. We don't go protesting their churches or beliefs."

"True," Iris agreed.

"What's through that door?" Serena pointed to the basement door.

"Storerooms and basement. Nothing interesting." I shrugged it off.

"Cool. I feel like this building is very old. Full of spirits and stories. Maybe I could research it. Maybe it was an old witch's shop? Someone who was killed?" she asked.

"I doubt it. It was built in the 1800s, not the 1600s. It's all brick, so it holds the history in the stone. You can research the land and what was here, certainly. It might be something, but the building isn't quite old enough for the witch trials." I liked the girl's spunk, but she seemed scattered. Poor Esme, trying to get her to focus on her magical studies.

"Could I get the tour?" she asked.

186

"Not now. I'm afraid we're doing inventory, and the basement area is a mess. You and the twins can hang out in the coven room or the reading nook on the second floor while it's quiet," I suggested.

Esme walked up from the basement, and I saw Serena freeze up. "Sorry, I have to go. More homework awaits."

Ellen walked up as Serena bolted out the door.

"Who is that girl?" Ellen asked.

"A friend from college," Violet answered.

"We're back to work, now. Don't worry," Iris added.

"I'm not worried. That girl left us a fifty-dollar tip. She can come back whenever she likes." Ellen grinned. The twins followed Ellen back to the counter.

"She knows how to make a good first impression," I said to Esme.

Esme walked up. "She was here?"

"Why? Isn't she allowed? The girl is what? Nineteen? She can come in for coffee," I said.

"Of course. I just usually keep my private lesson students away from here. I don't want them dropping in for help or bugging me while I'm working. Boundaries are good," she said.

Esme still looked rattled. "You can be mad about the truth potion all you want. Until you tell me the truth about myself, the secret, I won't even begin to apologize," I replied.

She shot me a look of disapproval.

Pick Your Potion

"If you were in my shoes, you'd do the exact same thing. You wouldn't stop until you found the truth. Neither will I." I shot her an icy stare.

"That doesn't involve Serena or Bran. That family is powerful. You don't want to cross them," she said.

"You wanted me to get involved with one of them. Now, I need to be careful? What is the deal?" I asked.

"Just be careful. Grow your powers. Don't spend so much time worrying about the past. Some secrets really don't matter, anymore," she said.

"I don't believe you for a second." I stalked off. Who could I totally trust, anymore? My nice little world felt much darker and more complicated than it did just a week ago.

Chapter Twenty

I felt a bit frumpy. Black sweater dress, purple tights, black boots and a black leather jacket. But it was cold outside. Showing skin wasn't an option. I wasn't ready for that anyway. I had a lot to talk to Bran about. But it felt more like a summit meeting about issues than a date. Good thing I hadn't mentioned it to Esme or my aunt. I met him at an Italian place on the other end of town.

"You look lovely," he said.

I took the single black calla lily he offered. "Thank you. Esme mentioned she's tutoring your cousin. I didn't want any of our family to get too excited or ahead of us. My cousins and yours are young enough to..."

"I understand. Esme never married, did she?" he asked.

"No." I followed the host who sat us in a private room. Bran took my coat and held my chair. This was a showing off date. Bran was impressing me.

"Champagne?" a waiter offered.

"No, thanks," I said.

"Burgundy wine?" Bran suggested.

"Just a little," I agreed.

The waiter handed us menus and poured the wine. "I'll give you a moment."

"You really didn't need to go this fancy, Bran," I said.

Pick Your Potion

"If I'm going to do something, I do it right." He sipped his wine.

"Why did you ask about Esme?" I asked.

He lifted a shoulder. "She might be living vicariously through you. She has a long life ahead of her but half of it being feline. I don't know how she does it."

"I don't either. I thought I wanted that when I was young, but I couldn't shift to feline in time. Now, I'm more relieved I didn't." I tried the wine. It was rich and earthy.

"I'm glad you didn't either. My cousin likes you, by the way. She mentioned talking to you at the café. If she gets under your feet or makes a pest of herself, let me know." He stared at the menu.

"She wasn't a pest. She knows the twins from school. She did rush off when she saw Esme, but no one wants to be cornered by a tutor when they're out with friends or getting coffee. I'm sure she'll settle in and get comfortable." I examined my options for dinner.

"I hope you're not a vegetarian," he said.

"No, I'm not. My aunt is so I can make a meal out of anything. But the Cajun chicken pasta looks good," I said.

"Not the prime rib?" he asked.

"I prefer my steak well done. I don't like to remember anything bled for me to eat. I'm not a vampire." I smiled.

"So, those rumors are false."

"You believed them?" I asked.

"No, you're far too hot-blooded for that. I'm sure they'll cook whatever you like however you like it." He set the menu aside. "I hope you don't believe the rumors about me."

"I'm not sure what the rumors about you are. Your family is old, wealthy, powerful, and reclusive. Esme says you're a homebody. I don't know much else, besides what you told me about your businesses." I sat back and waited for more.

"I'm actually quite boring. I like succeeding in business. I like when the magical world is calm and things are in order. I traveled over the summers with my parents. They moved to Ireland when my brother finished school. Couldn't pass up an old castle." He smiled.

I liked his smile. He cared for his family and wasn't ashamed of it. "Who could turn down a castle?"

"It'd be much easier to manage your hunter friend in a dungeon," Bran said.

The waiter showed up and took our order. I got the prime rib well done just to see his eyebrow arch.

Once we were alone again, I thought about a dungeon. "Do you really have a dungeon?"

"Want to see it?" he offered.

"I'm not sure. Is it empty?" I asked.

"For now, yes. Is he giving you more trouble?"

I shrugged. "He wants to leave. I want him to go. But there are issues. Finally, the cops are off of my back. We have the autopsy results for Mrs. O'Conner, so it was natural causes. I guess my spell was wrong. But I don't know if I trust that hunter. His case is hard to get details on. Killing a werewolf who is killing humans is one thing. But I don't think he's telling me the whole truth."

Pick Your Potion

"Is he bound to?" Bran asked.

"No, but if he did something really wrong, I don't want him out there as a danger to others. He landed in my basement, and I feel responsible. Why doesn't the paranormal world handle this? Why don't we have wizards or witches who hunt down vamps and weres who kill humans? We could handle it better," I said.

Bran nodded. "Gypsy hunters are a tradition of the human world. They protect humans from the paranormal. We could handle the bad ones if we chose to. But I'm not sure we want to make enemies of the gypsies. There are strong witches among their numbers. They always want to be apart from other humans and from us. It's complicated."

"Why don't vampires self-police or werewolves? Like humans?" I asked.

"Some say, because they were human once, they still think of themselves as human with a little more power. Some never asked for that to happen to them. Then again, the more powerful vampires and weres believe they have a right to live how they want to live. That their nature makes them hunters and killers. Those large groups go where the carnage is so they won't be noticed."

"Like war zones?" I asked.

He smiled. "War zones. Places with rampant illness. Gypsies live in a lot of places around the world, but they move on when things get too dangerous. They'll be out of that area before you hear the word refugees. They see three steps ahead. So, then, the vampires and weres are free to feed. To feast. My brother is fascinated by it. You'd love talking to him."

"I don't want details about the carnage. I employ a lot of vampires who don't want to hurt people. They have two options. Blood bank expired or butcher blood. They attack a human, and I'll stake them myself." I shook my head.

"And werewolves? Do you help them, too?" he asked.

"Sure. If they need a potion to keep them from changing, we provide it free. If they refuse the potion or it doesn't work on them, we lock them up for the nights of the full moon. That's why I have the cells in my basement. Occasionally, we catch a newbie who doesn't know they're a were. Once they do, they can make a plan and get the potion. It works on most of them. But now, I feel like we need to police the hunters who like their job too much. Go too far," I said.

Bran nodded. "I agree. I looked into your uncle and his family. Vin was well known, and people trusted him. He's mostly retired, now, and he deserves that. The gypsies do police themselves more or less. Your friend in the basement is not a gypsy."

"No. I wonder how some of them get into it. Like my dad," I said.

"Your dad was a hunter?" he asked.

I nodded. "But not a gypsy. I've asked a few times, but my aunt just falls apart. Losing her sister nearly killed her. But I don't feel like I know much about him."

"You were very young. I was, too. I don't know anything about your father, but I'm sure we could

Pick Your Potion

research it. If it will make you feel better. Sometimes digging in the past only causes pain," he said.

I nodded. "It would upset my aunt. I don't know. Maybe I'll feed that hunter a truth potion and see what he really did. I won't set a dangerous man loose on the world."

"Smart. If you need help, I'm around."

"Thanks. And if you need any help with Serena, I'm here. The twins are about the same age, and I'm used to it. I guess I should've asked if you have any sisters. I've only heard about the one brother," I said.

"Just the brother. So, girls are a bit different. Serena was spoiled. She's like Scarlet O'Hara. She'll get her way or make it her way. Her parents indulged her. She has a couple younger sisters who went with their parents. Serena wanted freedom and thought college would be it. Dorms and parties. Then, they stuck her in my custody. She needs direction and discipline."

"Wow. That's a handful. You'll put her in her place," I said.

He sipped his wine. "She's good deep down. She has the right intentions. But she doesn't always think things through. The consequences are what she needs to think about. Especially since she has magical powers. Her younger sisters aren't as gifted. Serena has powers and wasn't fully educated in how to handle them. I might need your help, as well as Esme's."

"You've got my help, but I'm not much of a teacher. Serena might have more powers than I do." I shrugged.

He stared at the wine bottle until it hovered over the table. He moved it over my glass and tipped it to refill my wine. I mentally grabbed the bottle and put it right side up and pushed back. I filled his glass then levitated the cork and plugged the wine bottle.

"Showoff," he said.

The door opened, and I hastily put the wine where it belonged as the waiter brought in our food.

Pick Your Potion

Chapter Twenty-One

I'd gone on some dates in my day, but none of them ended in brewing a potion. But the vampires had texted me that Ryan was trying to escape, again.

"It needs to be strong and last. He'll fight it," I said.

Bran tossed in another handful of herbs, and the mix smoked.

I stirred it and poured it into a large glass jar.

"Got it." I mixed in some iced tea. It was triple the potion I'd given to Esme. This time, I felt no guilt.

"Ready?" he asked.

I nodded. "You carry this. I'll have my phone recording."

Bran led the way, and I followed.

"Let me go. It's over. I heard them talking," Ryan said.

He paced the cell like a caged wolf.

"One thing first. Drink this," I said.

"What are you doing? I don't need a drink. I need to leave." Ryan pointed at the stairs.

"Who were you trying to call from my bedroom?" I asked.

"Mind your own business," he shot back.

"That's enough." Bran waved his hand and Ryan was pressed back against the wall of the cell. His mouth was awkwardly open.

Pick Your Potion

Bran levitated the jar of tea potion into the cell and poured some down Ryan's throat.

Ryan coughed and gagged.

"Drink it or we'll feed you more," I said.

He garbled a question as more tea was poured. Bran wasn't choking or waterboarding him. Ryan had chances to breathe.

When half was in, I touched Bran's shoulder. He pulled the jar back and waited.

"Ryan, how many people did you kill chasing that werewolf into the mall?" I asked.

Ryan shook his head. "Things happen."

"How many humans were killed? You killed the werewolf, fine. How many humans were dead when it was done?" I asked.

"Four. They got in the way. You can't leave witnesses. You don't understand." Ryan shook.

"You killed four people?" I said.

"No, four people were dead, in addition to the werewolf. I killed two. She killed two. They got in the way." Ryan glared at me.

"Who is she? Your sister?" I asked.

He shook his head. "She was special. I have to know she's okay. I can't find her. I can't get her on the phone. Her parents probably took her away. They never approved of me."

"This is new. You had a girlfriend? Was she arrested?" I asked.

He laughed. "No, I'm sure she's not arrested. She said to come here. Meet her here. But she hasn't come for me."

Bran and I exchanged a confused look. "Does she know to get in touch with my uncle?"

198

CC Dragon

"No, she said she could get in, and we'd be gone. She had money saved up. We'd be long gone and far away. But it's been too long. She's forgotten about me or her family caught her. Let me out, so I can find her." He kicked at the air.

"We could hand you over to the police, right now, so you better cooperate," Bran said.

"Oh, please do. Without her, my life means nothing." Ryan swatted at the jar.

"Who is this woman? What's her name?" I demanded.

He pursed his lips and shook his head.

"Tell me her name, and maybe I can help you. Maybe you'll both go to jail," I suggested.

"A jail couldn't hold her. She'd just leave. She'd be here taking me away if she really loved me." He gritted his teeth together.

"I want a name or you're not going anywhere," I said.

"Serena. Serena Murray." He fell to his knees, his shoulders slumped.

"What?" Bran snapped.

"He came up from the Carolinas," I said.

"She set this all up." Bran's fists clenched.

"Calm down." I grabbed Bran's shoulder. "I had no idea."

"No wonder she was asking about this place. The coven," he seethed.

"She killed two people. I think that's a bigger problem." I stopped recording.

"You know her? Bring her to me, please!" Ryan, now free from Bran's control, shook the door of the cell.

199

Pick Your Potion

"Bring her to you? Do you know who he is? She's his cousin. You're lucky he hasn't killed you, yet," I said to Ryan.

"She loves me. I love her," Ryan sighed.

"She's a witch. You're a human." Bran shook his head.

"We have to do something. They killed people. Innocent humans," I said.

Bran ran his hands through is hair. "She'd just escape a human jail with magic. She'll have to be handled by the witch's council. But him?"

"We can send him to jail. But if she loves him, she'll take him out. She was eyeing the door today. With me and Esme here, she's not the strongest witch. She couldn't take him from us. But a human jail—she could spring him," I said.

Bran looked at me intensely. "You didn't know?"

"Know? No! I had no idea he was connected to her. My uncle brought me a hunter who needed to hide out. It's happened more than once. They were never dating a witch. Or running from murdering innocent humans. He never said anything except about a sister. I don't know how to punish a witch or him for this." I wanted to call Esme.

"You were calling her? Trying to lure her here?" Bran asked Ryan.

Ryan nodded. "I had her cell number. A couple of them. I left her messages, but she never called me back. They wouldn't give me a phone. Esme took my burner phone." Ryan shot me an evil look.

200

"Because she's smart. If she'd trusted her instincts, she would've turned you over to the police, but we'll handle this better than humans. You might not think so, but we will make sure you don't hurt anyone, again." Bran waved at the cell.

Ryan's mouth moved, but we heard nothing.

"Nice soundproofing. What do we do with him?" I asked.

"Her first. We need to come up with a plan that's fair. Punishment. There is a system for this, but her parents would be furious if we turned her over to the witch's council. We handle it. She's under twenty-one, so she's not fully powered or considered an adult by the council. Murder."

I knew there was a council, but I had no idea their procedure for handing out justice.

"Come on; we need to go get her, now," Bran said.

"Wait. Just wait." I took his hand and led him back to the second floor. "She was asking about Mrs. O'Conner. Why would she threaten us? Were there any other threats against witches?" I said.

"She's protective. She's studying women's studies, and the witch trials are a big part of her focus," he said.

"Right. That might all be true, even though she moved here for him. She pulled all this out of nowhere when her parents were going to be gone...then she could chase down her boyfriend and run wild with him." I couldn't believe how clueless some men could be. "Serena seems sweet and clueless, but she might have set up all of this."

"Her magic needs work," he said.

Pick Your Potion

"Maybe, but her scheming is top notch. Maybe she wants more advanced lessons?" I asked.

"You think she made the threats against Mrs. O'Conner?" he asked.

"Esme was tutoring Serena. No doubt they got to talking about the incident at the shop. Maybe Serena wanted to impress Esme? Like she was standing up for witches everywhere? A few threats are nothing I'd put past a teen to do as a prank. We need to find out what she actually did. We need to find out any other crimes, to be sure. We might need more truth potion." I filled up the cauldron.

He nodded. "You're right. Serena would want to impress you and Esme. The two most powerful witches here are under attack. She'd love to be the one who rescued you. I never thought. She's too young for that sort of a Bonnie and Clyde romance, as well."

"Well, we'll get the truth out of her, and we can sit down with Esme and decide what to do about all of it," I said.

"No, not tonight. Invite her to a coven meeting tomorrow. Make it look normal. See if someone there threatened the old woman. See if anyone is helping the guy in the basement. Then, I can search her rooms and call her parents. See if they knew about him. See if she confesses to you and Esme." He shook his head.

"She doesn't know us that well." I shrugged.

"Serena has a romantic streak—she might try to play on your emotions. I just want the whole

CC Dragon

story before we try to settle on a punishment. See if she really loves that hunter jerk."

"What do we do with him? I'll give him to the cops, but if she lets him out..." I flopped on a sofa.

"That's why I don't want to rush. We need to get all the information." He sat next to me.

"Do we need to get her parents back here?" I asked.

He shook his head. "She's an adult as far as the human world is concerned."

"But we can punish her without her parents' permission? Or the council's?" I asked.

"The council will approve our punishment or amend it, but it'll be quieter than if we had a judge come and hear the evidence or we go there. Then, news will spread."

"Witch gossip?" I teased.

"Exactly. Just what my family doesn't want. Serena is smart when manipulating her family, but she's not brilliant with magic. She probably panicked and killed whoever that was at the mall when she meant to freeze them. I just want to make sure that's all she did." Bran nodded.

"I think we need some tea or wine. Too bad I don't have a liquor license here," I said.

He grabbed my hand and held it tight. "Thank you for your help."

I looked into his dark and caring eyes. "Thank you for yours. Crazy night."

"Fate tends to do that to us." He leaned over and kissed me.

I froze for a second, completely thrown off guard. But he was a good kisser...

203

Pick Your Potion

Chapter Twenty-Two

I called a coven meeting for the next evening. I told Esme to bring Serena, and Bran would make sure she came. The members assembled. It'd been hard not to quiz my cousin and aunt about the secret in my life. That was selfish and crazy. I'd lived this long without details. Right now, I had to make sure two murderers didn't escape justice.

Bran would slip into the café right when the coven meeting began. If he attended the meeting, Serena would know something was wrong. But if she tried to flee or take Ryan, he'd stop them.

When everyone was there, I stood, and the room got quiet. Serena stood next to Esme with the cousins on her other side. Serena looked around, but mainly, she was looking down her nose at the mix of people.

"I wanted to apologize to you guys. The police confirmed that it was natural causes. I'm not sure if my spell was wrong. The spell said it was unnatural causes, but there might have been other issues we don't know about. Mr. O'Conner is done with the protesting. The humans have a resolution, and I don't want to upset anyone by dragging it out to prove anything. But we would still like to find out who threatened Mrs. O'Conner. We don't want to be attacking humans for their ignorance or fear. The point of the café and this coven is to reach out and have good relations with humans. If anyone knows anything

Pick Your Potion

about who made those threats, I want to hear about it now," I said.

Serena scoffed.

"Excuse me?" I asked.

"Why do you care what humans think? They shouldn't be threatening what they don't understand. All their wars are out of ignorance and arrogance," Serena said.

"That doesn't mean we threaten them. We must set an example of order," Esme said.

"What do you even know about this, Serena? You're new here," I said.

"Who is she?" Ellen asked.

"Serena Murray. Of the Carolina Murrays." Serena flipped her hair.

I nearly laughed, but she was a lot more dangerous than she was spoiled. "She's a cousin of the Killeans, staying with them. Very recently. Have you meddled with anything, Serena?" I asked.

"Meddled? That old lady threatened your café and coven. I heard that through the witch network. What's wrong with a little warning that karma might get them? She threatened us. I threatened them," Serena said.

"You what?" Iris asked.

"I made a phone call. I had a friend make one, too, and leave a note. No big deal. The spell was just to bug her."

"Spell?" Bran asked from the door.

"You're supposed to wait downstairs," I said.

"I couldn't help listening in. What spell?" he demanded.

206

She jerked her chin. "Doesn't matter. She died too soon. The spell didn't work."

I cleared my throat. "We already know about the mall and the hunter. Tell us what spell you cast on Mrs. O'Conner."

"It doesn't matter. It was a joke. The mall was self-defense. A mistake. It went wrong." She waved it off.

"Repeat the spell," Bran said.

Serena flinched. "Teach this bitter old woman karma is real. Give her a mega dose of her own medicine so she knows how it feels."

"Mega dose of her own medicine?" I wanted to curse her out. The girl made a rookie mistake. Spells couldn't be ambiguous or the worst results always happened.

"What? She was a bitter old grouch. She deserved it. She wished bad things on you guys. She was mean to you, so she deserved people being mean to her for a bit. Karma." Serena shrugged.

"That woman died of an overdose of insulin." I pulled up the text on my phone from Detective Shelley. "They ran a glucose test, and she had no measurable sugar in her body. She took a mega dose of insulin and went to bed. Your spell worked and was taken literally," I said.

"No. That's crazy. I didn't know she was on medicine." Serena gasped.

"Bind her," someone called.

Esme waved a hand.

Serena tried to walk away and found herself frozen.

Pick Your Potion

"Let me go. I demand you let me go. It was natural causes. My spell was a flop. I didn't mean to kill her. I didn't kill her." Serena shrieked.

"What about the humans in the mall that you killed to save your hunter boyfriend?" I played the video of Ryan confessing.

She stared at the screen, and her face went red.

"That idiot!" she shouted.

"He was under a powerful truth potion," Bran said.

"He betrayed me. That bastard!" she screamed. Then, she took a deep breath and seemed to regroup. "It was all self-defense in the mall."

"You followed him here. You must care about him," I said.

"He pissed off my dad. Dad threatened him if he didn't stay away from me. I couldn't handle being separated from Ryan. Especially when he went on a dangerous hunt. It was late, and he was going to take out the werewolf and be done. I went for backup. We didn't know there were humans in there doing late inventory. They surprised us. It was an accident." She bounced.

I laughed. She'd tried to stomp her foot but was frozen from the elbows down.

"Accident or not, you killed two humans that night. He did, as well. You both have to pay. Plus Mrs. O'Conner, goofed spell or not. We can call in a rep from the witch's council or handle it ourselves," Esme said.

"She is young," my aunt added.

"We will handle it and inform the council, but the punishment will be severe. You're all invited to the Killean mansion tonight at midnight. We will set down punishment at that point. For her and the hunter. She's my cousin and my responsibility. The hunter came here because Serena knew she could get here and had a place to stay. She thought she could rescue him from hiding. They're my problem," Bran said.

"They became our problem, big time. Thanks," my aunt said.

"I'm sorry. I had no idea any of this was going on. I'll be talking to Serena's parents before we pass judgment. I'm sorry you ladies had to deal with this." He glared at his cousin.

"We? Who is we?" Serena asked.

"Claudia's business was almost ruined because of you. She had to babysit your boyfriend. They patched him up. You've been trying to get in here since you arrived in town, and now, I know why. A human hunter with no self-control. Claudia and I will decide what the consequences are. Esme, Claudia and I will collectively cast the spells needed so we can't undo it unless we all agree. Fair enough?" he asked.

I nodded. Esme and my aunt nodded, as well.

"No! That's crap. You can't touch Ryan!" she shouted.

"Oh, yes, we can. Or I could hand him over the South Carolina police, along with his confession. Would you like that better?" I asked.

"We could turn you over to the police for that, too," Iris said. "Murderer."

Pick Your Potion

"Like I'd stay in jail. If I can kill someone with a remote spell, I'm obviously really strong. So, I'll overcome whatever you do to me." She struggled against Esme's binding spell.

I stepped up to the bratty little witch. "I really thought you were interesting. Your major. Your focus. It was all a lie to get into my café and my coven. To get your boyfriend back. What was the plan once you got him out of my basement? Run off and go on a killing spree?"

"No, I never wanted to kill anyone. Our plans were none of your business." She sneered at me. "He'd do anything for me. You have no idea what that's like. Poor single witch and her coffee shop with her hippie aunt and her friend who lives life like a cat more than a human. And those twins. How do you stand it? Surrounded by so many dull, boring humans. You have real powers, Claudia." She shook her head at me.

"I'll take good humans over murderous witches any day." I looked at Bran. "Can you contain her at home? I don't want to put her downstairs with Ryan."

"She won't get away from me. See you at midnight." He leaned over and kissed my cheek.

I tried not to blush. In a flash, he and his cousin were gone.

"What was that?" Violet asked.

"Nothing. He's forward. We had one date," I said.

"Looks like a good one," my aunt said.

"It was nice enough until we had to interrogate Ryan with a truth potion. Not exactly normal," I said.

210

"But you're a good team," Esme said.

I shot her a look but shook off the scrutiny. If Bran and I worked out, we worked out. If not, we could still be good allies.

"Can we watch?" Ellen asked.

"No, Esme and I can handle Ryan. We'll have enough witnesses and send the punishment to the council. They will no doubt approve it, but any alterations can be made quickly. Thank you, everyone, thanks for being here. It is good to know I wasn't crazy," I said.

"You were right, but that hunter... Vinny will want to kill him," my aunt said.

"Well, he can't. Even if we hand him in to the police, he wouldn't get a death penalty. At most, it'd be manslaughter. We'll give him a better lesson our way." I flopped into a big chair as the coven meeting broke up.

"Your silence and support is appreciated, ladies," Esme said.

Iris and Violet stood in front of me. "That girl is crazy," they said.

"I don't want you spending too much time with her." I rubbed my forehead.

"Is she going to be free to roam around?" my aunt asked.

"Bran and I have to finalize the punishment. Now, we know she killed Mrs. O'Conner, as well. How could she be so reckless with her spells?" I sighed.

"I'm glad to see you're working with Bran." Esme smiled.

Pick Your Potion

The twins grinned. My aunt nodded. So much for my private life staying private until I figured out if there was any future in it.

Chapter Twenty-Three

Esme and I arrived around nine p.m. with Belle as another witness. She was a gypsy witch but a powered witch nonetheless and independent of my coven. Ryan was less cooperative, but he couldn't do much against our magic bindings. A young handsome man answered the door. A butler? Really?

"We're here to discuss the sentences of the criminals," I said.

"Miss Crestwood, please. Esmeralda." The butler bowed.

"This is Belle Andrews," I informed him.

"The master is in his library. The other criminal is being held in the solarium." He led the way.

We all followed and found ourselves in the solarium. Serena was still immobilized and shouted against her invisible bonds. Esme moved Ryan next to her so they could see each other, but both were bound in their own spells so they couldn't touch or even hear each other.

Ryan's anguish was clear, but they needed to understand what they had done was wrong. There were consequences, even if the human world couldn't prove it or understand what happened. They called Mrs. O'Conner's death natural. That gave them peace. But we couldn't let these two get away with their crimes.

I turned and the butler was gone.

Pick Your Potion

"I feel underdressed," Belle said.

"Don't worry about it." I was in jeans and a sweater. Nothing fancy about me.

"Ladies, welcome," Bran said as he walked in.

The guy was still in a suit and looked at ease. Dark hair, dark eyes, and handsome features—I could do worse. He was definitely worth spending time with. Friends or more, who knew, right now

"We need to talk about what punishment we'll hand down," Esme said.

"Agreed. Well, my cousin's parents are very concerned that she deceived them. They won't be back until next year but have trusted me to hand down whatever sentence I see fit and to oversee her custody. I'd like to hear your thoughts on punishment first," he said.

I studied the cocky girl. "Bind her powers for three years. No magic. Restrict her to school, your home, and a charity place to volunteer and other acceptable close-by places only. Make her volunteer. Make her go to school. Coven meetings should be mandatory. Continue her work with Esme so she understands spells before she can use them, again. All of that for a year and then assess if she is ready for more freedom to see if she can be trusted and has learned."

"Three years without magic?" an older man asked as he walked up.

"Ladies, my cousin Vern—a vampire," Bran introduced.

"Hello," I said. "Yes, three years. One for every human she killed. In the third year, maybe we could restore some basic powers to see if she

214

CC Dragon

uses them responsibly. But she'd need to be closely monitored. Like parole."

"Magical parole." Belle smirked.

"She has to be held accountable," Esme said.

"Did I miss anything?" a handsome young man asked as he entered.

"My other cousin, Harry. He's a werewolf," Bran said.

"Claudia, Esme, and Belle. All witches," I said.

Harry bowed and smiled. He locked eyes with me for a split second, and I felt an odd tingle but then Harry stared at Belle.

"I'm a gypsy witch," Belle said.

"What about the hunter? He killed the werewolf. That's okay. But two humans?" Vern shook his head at the trapped man.

"Killing werewolves isn't okay," Harry said. "There are wolf runs and natural packs where wolves can run free from humans and hunters. He could've captured the werewolf and relocated him to a sanctuary," Harry said.

"As long as they don't attack humans, witches, or wizards—that's fine," I agreed.

Esme cleared her throat to keep us on track. "I think Ryan needs at least two years of imprisonment. He knew his job, and that it wasn't a free pass to accidentally kill anyone. Even if it was involuntary manslaughter, there have to be consequences. But he and his girlfriend were on a spree of some sort. He was impressing her with his werewolf hunting skills."

"Imprison him where? Not in my basement," I said.

"We have a dungeon," Bran replied.

215

Pick Your Potion

"A legit, guarded dungeon?" I asked.

"Would you like the tour? We have time before midnight," Bran offered.

"I would," Belle said.

"I'll go on faith, for now. I prefer to keep an eye on them," Esme said.

"I'll stay," Vern said.

Harry offered his arm to Belle. She blushed and stuck near me.

"I'll go, too," I said.

We followed the men.

"I'm sorry," Belle said and looked at me.

"No need," Harry said.

"Harry, I'm not sure how much you know about the gypsy culture. Belle is a Romanichal Gypsy, and unmarried women aren't allowed socialize with single men. Certainly not touch them. Most girls marry very young, but Belle is a rebel. She pursued a career and helps people, but her reputation is still important," I said.

"How fascinating. How are you two related?" Harry asked.

"My aunt married a gypsy man. Belle is his second cousin. We became friends as kids. I'm a bad influence." I grinned.

"No, you saved me. I would've run off rather than marry young. You showed some of the gypsies that Gorger girls could be good and close to the family and have a job." She loosened her grip on my arm and walked a bit faster.

"Gorger?" Harry asked.

"Non-gypsy," I filled in.

"I can't wait to see this gypsy wedding," Bran said.

216

CC Dragon

"You're bringing him?" Belle asked.

"Why not? He's never been to one. It'll be a cultural experience," I said.

"He'll think we're trash," Belle whispered.

"No, he won't. He'll ask a lot of questions. Don't be ashamed of where you came from. You don't have to marry a gypsy, but you are one." I patted her arm and walked ahead with Bran.

The dungeon lived up to its name. Dark and cold, the walls were rock, and there were no windows. Bran conjured a light ball, and I did the same as we wound through the corridors. Finally, a large room opened. There were cells separated by rock walls. A man stood taller when he saw Bran.

"A guard, even," I said.

"I employ a few vampires myself. My family is old and reclusive. We aren't perfect or sweet. Humans fear us. But we are generally good. The few exceptions who are disturbed or evil are housed here," Bran said.

Belle and Harry walked along. I hung back.

"You don't want to see?" Bran asked.

"Your family isn't a freak show. I'm sorry you have to do this to any of them," I said.

"At least look at an empty cell to be sure you're okay with Ryan staying here for two years. We don't deny quality food, clean water, or health care. Entertainment and luxuries are restricted," Bran said.

I walked by a full cell to an empty one.

"I see it. I see the animal. Get it out!" the old man shrieked from the occupied cell.

217

Pick Your Potion

Harry waved it off. "He doesn't like werewolves. He has the sight, but no control over his mind or mouth."

I nodded and looked in an empty cell. It was dark and gloomy, but the bed looked fairly comfortable. There was a small desk along with a sink and toilet in one corner. It wasn't overly cramped.

"What do they do for showers? What do they do all day?" I asked.

Bran smiled. "If they cooperate, there is a shower down the hall. If they try to run, they can use the sink in their cell plus soap and a washcloth. There is a drain in the floor. It's set up so we don't take them out if they can't be trusted. "

I nodded.

"As for what they do all day? They can request books from the library. But I think Ryan would benefit from some looped video rehab," Harry said.

"Rehab?" Belle asked.

"There are people who want peace between werewolves and humans. To stop the hunting and create a better dialogue," Harry replied.

"They should only be hunting werewolves who murder and refuse to take measures during the full moon. We have potions or confinement," I said.

"Some werewolves want an island to themselves. Just werewolves. So they can roam free and enjoy the shift. Fight, play, and mate," Harry said.

"Mate?" Belle said softly.

218

I smiled at Bran. "I've no objection to that sort of thing. I can't imagine all werewolves would want that. Plenty have human family, as well as were family."

"But is this acceptable?" Bran asked as he gestured to the empty cell.

"I think so. Thank you for offering to house them," I said.

"Shouldn't Serena get some time down here too?" Belle asked.

I nodded. "I think so. Even just a week or two to scare her."

"Her parents wouldn't like it," Harry said.

"Tough. They've entrusted her to me. I think a week down here will scare her. Show her how bad the punishments could be." Bran checked his watch. "We should go up."

We made our way back to the solarium. An old wizard stood before the two criminals.

"Ladies, my great uncle Dutch. He is the family peacekeeper. He'll record the crimes, the punishments, and take it to the witch's council for approval."

Dutch bowed. "The reading of the charges."

As he droned on, I looked up at Bran.

"What?" he whispered.

"That kiss on the cheek at the coven meeting. Now, people think things," I whispered back.

"Good. It was important to stake a claim before the other men in my family met you. My brother is dashing. My cousin is handsome." He nodded.

"And Vern is eternal?" I teased.

Pick Your Potion

He grinned. "Exactly. You can end things whenever you like, but I won't have any men in my family moving too fast and snapping you up while I'm taking my time."

"I'm not one to rush things either. But, at the wedding, you will meet my uncle who has heard about that kiss," I warned him.

"I'll handle him," he said.

"Gypsy men fight dirty. A lot. Just so you know." I was trying to find a way to say be on your guard without making it sound like I thought he couldn't handle a fight. Of course, he could; he was a wizard.

"I can handle myself without magic if I have to. But I don't intend to fight with anyone," he said.

"Good plan," I giggled.

"Shh," Esme whispered.

"Now, the accused have a chance to speak briefly. To beg for mercy or deny a charge. First, Serena." The old wizard waved at her.

The soundproofing came off.

"Please let me go. Bran, please. They were accidents. Things happened too fast at the mall. I was scared. And I got the spell all wrong. I never meant to kill anyone. But I need to learn, not be punished," Serena cried.

The old wizard waved at her, and her voice was silenced. Then, Ryan could be heard.

"Let me out of here. You have no authority over me!" he shouted.

"Want to be handed over to the police? You still have warrants. You can go into the prison system," I said.

He glared at me and began yelling threats.

The old wizard waved at Ryan to silence him.

"Both of you have been accused of ending human lives when your lives were not in imminent danger. That is illegal in the magical and human realm. The proposed penalty for each of you is as follows..."

The old wizard read over what we'd discussed.

"You're sure you want to go to a gypsy wedding?" I whispered in Bran's ear.

"I want to see you in a fancy dress and have a new cultural experience. The Equinox Ball will be fun for you," he whispered back.

True, it was a fair trade of experiences. I couldn't wait to see his face when he saw the brides' dresses.

"If anyone present does not agree that these consequences are fair, please declare your objection, now," the old wizard said.

The silence was clear.

"The sentences are passed. There will be three members who cast the spell so it can't be undone by one person." The old wizard waved us up.

Bran, Esme, and I focused on Serena first. The energy from our three spells wove red and green lights around the girl. We finished with her and worked on Ryan. Blue lights zipped around him until the spell took full hold.

The wizard had us sign a scroll and then disappeared.

"That was quick," Belle said.

The old wizard returned. "Approved."

"That was quicker." Harry laughed.

Pick Your Potion

"No objections?" Esme asked.

"No, they did think you could be harder on the girl. A week in the dungeon could be a month instead, but they left that to family discretion because she is under twenty-one. I'll put this in the family files. We take custody of Ryan and Serena." The old wizard bowed to us. "Ladies."

He disappeared and so did the two criminals.

I felt odd. Ryan had been in my basement for so long that I felt responsible. Part of it was relief, but I also felt like I'd failed to fully understand who I had living in my building. He could've killed vampires or hurt humans. I was lucky it wasn't worse.

"You okay?" Belle asked.

"Fine. Just glad it's over. Justice for Mrs. O'Conner and those humans at the mall." I sighed.

"We have a midnight snack set up in the small library. Tea, cheese, crackers, cake, and wine," Harry said.

"I could use a bite," Belle said.

Esme stared at the empty space where Ryan had just been.

"You okay?" I asked her.

"I need to see the dungeon, now," she said.

Vern nodded. "I'll take her. You kids go get a snack."

We walked into the small library, which was a huge library to me, and there were footmen dressed to serve. I wanted the full tour.

A girl could get used to servants and a dungeon.

Epilogue

The new reality of no one in my basement and no murder to solve set in. It was nice. But now, I had a secret to uncover. The cousins played dumb. I hadn't worked up the courage to confront my aunt, just yet. We had a gypsy wedding to attend, and she always felt out of place there. Of course, Vinny's family all wished he'd married a gypsy girl.

Esme wouldn't discuss the secret, at all. The truth potion had put up a wall between us.

So, I went to the gypsy connection. Belle and her sister Vivian both worked; they lived with and supported their widowed mother. Their dad had been pretty awful so no one in the community mocked them for being old maids. They were both gorgeous girls who could've been married as teens but they didn't want to end up with a guy who was nice but turned into a drunk or worse later on. I couldn't blame them. Uncle Vin had been called to help handle their father when he'd gotten out-of-control drunk. I'd overheard some of those stories when Vin told Aunt Mandy about it.

The gypsy sisters and I met for lunch at a burger place near their employment. Vivian worked in the morgue at the hospital. She kept the zombie population down by pushing a needle into each deceased person's ear until she hit brain matter. No one noticed, but a zombie outbreak? We'd notice that!

Pick Your Potion

"Belle said Bran is hot and rich," Vivian said.

"He is. And he's nice. Ethical. Smart. So far, he's nice. You'll meet him at the wedding," I said.

We placed our orders, and I sipped a strawberry lemonade.

"What did you want to talk about if not Bran?" Belle asked.

"Did you want to talk about Harry?" I asked.

"Harry?" Vivian asked.

"A werewolf cousin of Bran's. He flirted with your sister," I said.

"He was nice, but we didn't talk or anything, really. I don't even know what he does for a living," she said.

"The Killeans own a lot of businesses. I can find out. Ask Bran at the wedding," I said.

"We can't approach a single guy," Belle said.

Vivian rolled her eyes. "He'll be with Claudia in a public place. Stop being so old-fashioned."

"What did you want to talk about?" Belle asked.

"Fine. I found out from Esme somehow that there is a secret about me or my childhood that I don't know. No one will tell me."

"Truth potion?" Viv suggested.

"I tried it. Whatever promises or vows they made to others are stronger than a truth potion. You two haven't heard anything?" I asked.

Belle shook her head. "Your parents were killed by a werewolf. Vin saved you and raised you."

"And my dad wasn't a gypsy hunter?" I asked.

"No, we understood he came to it from a family attack. That's how Gorger hunters usually get into the work. They were attacked or someone they loved was attacked, and they get in the hunter network. They tend to be loners. It's a bit unusual. It was said he was friends with Vin. A responsible hunter who respected gypsy culture. They ended up married to sisters, so they were family. Vin is the one who took the heat for not marrying gypsy. Everyone spoke wonderfully about your mother. We were told to be very nice to you because of what you went through," Viv said.

"Viv," Belle said.

"What? She wants the raw truth of what we were told. What we know. We weren't allowed to play with a lot of non-gypsy kids, but you needed friends and people who weren't going to ask questions about your dead parents. I know your aunt homeschooled you for a year until you were ready to go back. Then, you seemed to be okay. You came out of the fog." Viv smiled.

"Thanks for telling me the truth. Did anyone say it was my dad's fault or blame anyone? My mother always liked the darker side of things. She wanted to help everyone. And got too close to the weres and vamps, some said," I added.

"You do, too. But you have a system to help them and bring them to you. You don't go into the dark dens of a traditional werewolf pack or visit a vampire nest. You learned from her. None of it was her fault. Or your fathers. Or Vin's. There is a reason for hunters, no matter what Harry said," Belle said.

"Harry doesn't believe in hunters?" Viv asked.

Pick Your Potion

"We didn't get to talk about it much," Belle said.

"Some weres think they should be free to shift and be natural in certain areas. Boundaries set up. Hunt smaller animals. Like a wolf would. I don't know how I feel about that. Or how it could be monitored. But if someone said I couldn't practice magic because I lived in a human world and had humans in and out of my coffee shop, I'd fight that," I admitted.

"As long as they don't kill humans. There is a reason gypsies have been tasked to be hunters for generations. Our men can handle the dark side and a good fight. If they want to hunt deer or bunny rabbits, fine. Not humans," Viv said.

"Agreed," I said.

"We can ask around," Bell said. "See if Mom or anyone knows anything. They won't tell you but us, maybe they will."

"Thanks so much. A death where hunters and werewolves were involved, someone in the gypsy community will know. But who knows what the secret is? It might be something totally different." I sighed.

We sat back as our food was delivered. I grabbed the ketchup.

"I want to hear more about Harry," Viv said.

The look on Bran's face as we waited in the church said it all. The gypsy girls were dressed to party and the men to drink. Bran and Vin were the only two men in full suits other than the grooms, but that was okay.

226

I was in a silver dress that shimmered, but it was nothing like what the gypsy brides would be wearing.

"I feel like I'm lacking some rhinestones," he said to me.

My cousins laughed. "Men don't bling. Not like this." Iris pointed as the doors opened.

The brides couldn't fit down the aisle at the same time. Ten-foot wide fully hooped skirts narrowed to tiny waists. The bling was on the bodices, and both girls wore crowns. One dress was done in red, the other green. The trains went on and on.

"Those dresses have to weigh more than they do," Bran said in my ear.

I nodded. "They'll change for the dancing. The trains Velcro off."

"I've never seen anything like that," he admitted.

After the ceremony, we went to the hall adjacent to the church, and the bling only got bigger. The cakes had sparkles. The brides danced in the full gowns and cut the cake before disappearing. They came back in short skirts with bling all over.

The dancing kicked up and so did the drinking. Bran ditched his jacket and rolled up his sleeves to look less formal.

"Why are the young girls only dancing with each other?" he asked.

"Because if they dance with, boys their fathers will kill them. Until they're out and looking for husbands, there's no contact with boys. Some

Pick Your Potion

girls break the rules, but this family is strict and old school." I smiled.

"The dancing is very suggestive." Bran looked at me instead of the dance floor. "They're very young."

"Gypsy kids are never kids. The little boys are little men, and the girls are women, always looking to get married. It's their culture. But I'm glad I can dance with you and not get in trouble." I pulled him on the dance floor.

We weren't wild, but we did get noticed. The brides came over and dragged me to the DJ.

"You have to sing something," the red bride said.

"No, no, it's your wedding. You're the stars." I didn't show off my singing voice much. Never outside the family. But they knew I could carry a tune well enough.

"I have to see this," Bran said.

"It's our day. You have to," insisted the green bride.

"Fine." I took the microphone from the DJ. "The song from *Pulp Fiction* about the teenage wedding."

He gave me a thumbs up.

I walked to the front. "At the request of both beautiful brides, I'm going to sing something. Get ready to show off your twisting skills..."

The crowd went wild, and then, even the little kids were twisting like pros. I knew my audience. I couldn't sing as low as Chuck Berry, but I saw my aunt and uncle get up and dance, as well as my cousins. Bran stood at the back and grinned as everyone got lost in the music. I wasn't a gypsy witch, but I loved my gypsy cousins, and no one could party like they could. I hoped the teenage weddings would last, and Bran and I might have a shot, too.

For a few minutes, I was lost in song and forgot about the secret. Tomorrow. I'd get back on that investigation tomorrow.

A Note from the Author

Hi! Welcome to the world of strong witches, hot wizards, were, vamps, gypsies and more! If you enjoyed Pick Your Potion, please leave a review where you purchased it or on Goodreads.

Don't be shy! Let me know what you want more of Claudia and her vamps. The reclusive Killean clan. The gypsies...

Want more Cozy Paranormal Mysteries?

Check out the Deanna Oscar Series:

Book 1 *A Mansion, A Drag Queen, And A New Job*
Book 2: A Club, An Imposter, And A Competition
Book 3: *A Bar, A Brother, And A Ghost Hunt*

Keep your eye out for *Witch's Brew Cozy Mystery 2: Spells to Die For*

About the Author

A loyal Chicago girl who loves deep dish pizza, the Cubs, and the Lake, CC Dragon is fascinated by mysteries, sleuthing, as well as the supernatural.

CC loves creating characters, especially amateur sleuths who solve crimes in their spare time. A coffee and chocolate addict who loves fast cars, she's still looking for a hero who likes to cook and clean...so she can write more!

Website:
www.ccdragon.com

Facebook:
www.facebook.com/ccdragonauthor

Twitter:
www.twitter.com/authorccdragon

Goodreads:
www.goodreads.com/author/list/12051908.CC_Dragon

Newsletter:
app.mailerlite.com/webforms/landing/o6l4f0

Made in the USA
Columbia, SC
23 August 2018